Chameleon Assassin
Book 1 in the Chameleon Assassin Series

By BR Kingsolver

brkingsolver.com

Cover art by Heather Hamilton-Senter
www.bookcoverartistry.com

Copyright 2016 BR Kingsolver

⊕|⊕|⊕

License Notes

⊕|⊕|⊕

Other books by BR Kingsolver

The Telepathic Clans Saga
The Succubus Gift
Succubus Unleashed
Broken Dolls
Succubus Rising
Succubus Ascendant

And in 2017
Chameleon Uncovered

ACKNOWLEDGEMENTS

Valentina, as always, for your time, encouragement and edits. Heather for the gorgeous cover. A special thanks to Dee, Jackie, Jessica, Mia, and Michelle for reading my draft and offering suggestions. The book is much better due to your help. To all of you, a sincere thank you.

⊕⊕⊕

Table of Contents

CHAPTER 1

I crouched in the shadows as the watchmen strolled past. If they'd patrolled the way they were supposed to, most of the perimeter would have always been covered. But even watchmen got lonely. It was more companionable for them to walk together, covering both of their territories.

Fine with me. It left several stretches of wall unguarded for five minutes at a time, and cameras didn't cover a couple of those areas.

The watchmen turned the corner. I counted to twenty, then walked across the open street to the wall surrounding the Carpenter estate. My grappling hook caught the top of the ten-foot wall. I scampered up the rope and clamped two devices on the electrified barbed wire, then cut the wire between the devices.

I slithered over the wall, not sure whether to laugh or snarl at the broken glass embedded in its top. It didn't bother me because the Kevlar woven into my sweater kept it from penetrating. It was just the idea of it. The leap past the pressure plates in the ground near the wall made for a rough landing. Tuck and roll.

Someone as rich as Khalil Carpenter should have spent the money to upgrade his systems, not to mention hiring additional guards. No guards inside the wall, not even dogs. I guessed he thought he was saving money. It would have been cheaper to hire someone like me to fix it all. Instead, he took a chance that could land him in bankruptcy.

I adjusted my filter mask to make sure it still had a tight fit. Even that far out of the city, the air pollution was still toxic and hazardous on the lungs. You had to get hundreds of miles from civilization to find anything you could call clean air.

Bypassing the door alarm on the second floor balcony took less than a minute. The air inside was far better and I took off my filter mask.

Hacking into the computer in the study took five minutes, and installing the chip I brought with me took another minute.

Assignment complete.

Out of curiosity, I cracked the safe behind the small Picasso, scanned the dozen or so chips inside, and attached their contents to the data stream uploading to offsite from Carpenter's computer.

I slipped out of the study and headed toward the upstairs bedroom. The contract paid well, but the potential for a lot bigger payday was too tempting.

The sound of footsteps sent me scooting into the shadows. I stood next to a wall and used my chameleon mutation to blend into my surroundings. A woman walked past carrying an armload of towels and went up the stairs. I assumed she was one of the maids. She wore a black dress with a white belt and shoes. Maybe that was a uniform, but it was difficult to tell. I studied her closely until she was out of sight, then followed her.

The maid took the towels into a room, the master bedroom, according to the plans I had studied. Lousy timing. If she had taken too long, I would've had to abandon my plan. Lady luck favored me. The maid came out after only a couple of minutes carrying a bundle that I guessed were used towels. I had watched the Carpenters leave for dinner and the theater an hour before I climbed the wall. Of course, they would need fresh towels when they returned home. It would be yucky to use the same towel twice without washing it.

Rich people. In parts of the city, people were lucky if they had water clean enough to drink, let alone wasting it to wash.

I entered the bedroom and looked around. More a suite than a room. Sitting room, bedroom, two bathrooms, two dressing rooms, and a morning porch-slash-balcony, where the lord and lady of the manor might have breakfast. The bedroom was as large as my entire townhouse. Big enough to invite forty of their closest friends over for an orgy. Paintings on the walls, expensive rugs on the floors. Where would they hide a safe?

I searched the suite and checked Mrs. Carpenter's dressing room but didn't find anything. I finally found what I was searching for in what I assumed was Khalil's dressing room, behind a framed photograph of him on some tropical beach. The safe was ridiculously easy to crack, and the jewelry inside it was simply ridiculous. I might soon be able to buy my own country.

In five minutes, the servants would get off work and go home. I recalled the features and dress of the woman I'd seen, then stood in front of a mirror and imagined that I looked like her. Even after twenty years of doing it, it still amazed me to watch myself morph into someone else. I donned my filter mask, walked out of the bedroom, down the stairs, out the front door, and through the front gate toward the small parking lot where the servants rode a private bus into town. The guards barely glanced at me. I blurred my image as I walked by the bus and kept going until I reached my motorcycle.

⊕⊕⊕

Most mutations are small or innocuous. Scientists think that blond hair, red hair, and blue eyes originated as mutations. Major mutations are often fatal.

Beginning in the twentieth century, scientists began seeing an increase in mutations and developmental abnormalities. As the ozone layer depleted and worldwide radiation levels skyrocketed after the series of wars in the twenty-first century, such incidents increased.

By the time I was born, two out of ten babies had ambiguous sexual identities, two out of ten were born sterile, and two out of ten had identifiable mutations. Obviously, some of these categories overlapped, but that didn't take into account people like me and Mom, who had fairly radical mutations that no one could see. Dad estimated that more than half of all mutations were never documented.

My mutations were mild compared to those of the pseudo-vampires and lycanthropes, though evidence existed that the lycans' and similar mutations were enhanced through genetic engineering. Some of the psychic mutations were downright scary. And then there were the induced mutations, such as people with gills, who lived in the Pacific Ocean. I always thought it would be neat to live underwater.

⊕|⊕|⊕

I really wanted to show the jewelry to Dad, but I needed to stop by Mom's place first, since she set up the contract for the Carpenter job. I rode my motorcycle back to the city and into the business district.

Mom's hotel was on the edge of where the

4

business district met the entertainment district. To the east were the mutant ghettos. People tended to congregate with their own kind. Vampires lived with other vampires; lycanthropes lived with others who shared their mutations. Most vamps and some lycans could blend into normal society. The further east, the more noticeable and debilitating the mutations and the poorer the people.

I loved my mother, and I would never want anyone to think I was passing any kind of judgement on her or was ashamed of her. But I also never wanted anyone to think that I worked in her business.

A block from Mom's place of business, I ducked into an alley. A tall, slender blonde girl dressed all in black morphed into a voluptuous redhead in a low-cut white blouse and a black miniskirt. Most of Mom's employees thought that was how I really looked, like she did when she was my age.

Lilith's Palace was similar to a luxury boutique hotel, the kind of place where corporate types met their mistresses. The restaurant was exquisite, and I worshipped the chef as a god. The difference between her place and a normal hotel was that Lilith's provided a girl or two, or a boy, or both if you liked, along with the room.

Mike, the bouncer at the main entrance, showed his fangs in a grin when he saw me.

"Hey, Lizzie. How ya been? Ain't seen ya round here much lately."

"I was here yesterday, Mike," I told him as I took off my filter mask. "I just haven't been around on your shift. A girl needs her beauty sleep."

"Daylight's bad for ya," he said. "Causes cancer."

I didn't know about cancer, but sunlight was bad for people with his particular mutation. The sun didn't destroy vampires as in the legends, but they were extremely photosensitive.

"Life causes cancer, Mike. Lilith around?"

"Back in the office."

I wandered through the parlor and the bar, trying to ignore the men who hit on me. I hadn't entered the Palace in my own form since one of Mom's customers approached me on the street when I was twelve.

Mom's "Yes?" came when I knocked.

"It's me."

She opened the door and frowned. "I wish you wouldn't use that form," she said as she stepped aside and let me into the room.

I think seeing me as a younger version of her made her feel old. She was still beautiful at forty-five, with thick red hair, sparkling blue eyes and the kind of body women paid money for. Everything about her was natural, though, except her name. It was really Letitia, not Lilith, and Dad called her Lettie.

I shrugged. "All your employees know me like this. It's easier."

"I suppose," she said, motioning me to a chair. She settled into the chair behind the desk. "Would you like a drink?"

I shook my head.

"The data feed is working fine. What was that extra data bundle you sent?"

"Chips I found in his office safe. I didn't look at the data on the chips, just copied it and put the chips back where I found them."

She nodded. "I'll evaluate the data in the morning. That wasn't included in the contract, but if it's worth anything, I'll offer them to our customer first. And if they don't want them, I'll auction them off."

6

Mom leaned across the desk and handed me a payment card. I pressed it against my phone, waited for the money to transfer, then handed it back. One hundred thousand credits for hacking Carpenter's computer and installing a Trojan chip that transmitted everything he did to a rival corporation. I didn't know how much Mom made on the deal, and I didn't care. I had asked for a hundred grand and they paid it. I didn't know or care who the customer was, and they didn't know who I was or how we tapped into the data feed. They paid for results and we delivered.

Mom had been a corporate cyber security expert— defender and hacker. She was good enough at it, and gorgeous enough, that people were willing to overlook the inconvenient daughter she insisted on taking everywhere she went. I started learning computers when I was three. By the time I got to university, I could have taught some of my courses.

One day she decided she was tired of being a kept woman, quit her corporate job, left her executive vice president sugar daddy, and bought an old hotel on the edge of the business district. What she did with it raised a few eyebrows. I hadn't seen my grandparents since.

I had two mutations. From my mother, I inherited the ability to disrupt electrical currents, and electric shocks didn't affect me. Some mutants could deliver a shock, like an electric eel. I wasn't one of them, but they couldn't hurt me. If I stuck my finger in a light socket, the light shorted out. I was grateful that neither of my parents drowned me when I was young. Before I learned to control myself, anything electrical that I touched turned into a disaster. By the time I reached puberty, I learned to turn "it" on and off when I wanted to. "It" meaning totally screwing up any electrical current or device.

My other mutation was extremely rare. I was a chameleon. Not only could I blend into any background, I could also mimic other people or animals. I didn't physically change into their form, and I didn't feel any different. I just thought about looking different, and I appeared to take on another form. Once, Dad put sensors on my body, and they didn't report any changes when I morphed, but he and Mom said they could actually feel the differences in my size and shape, not just see them.

The mimicry could be face and body, but it could only be my clothes. I didn't have to brush my hair and put on makeup in the morning, I could just imagine I did and that was what people saw. Mom and Dad said it was a psychic thing, that I was projecting an illusion. They couldn't explain why cameras saw the same thing people did. If it were an illusion, you'd think the camera would still see me as me.

I didn't understand how it worked, but it was a very handy thing for a thief.

"You're awfully quiet tonight," she said.

"Tired, Mom. It takes a little more effort to break into an armed compound than simply doing a cyber attack."

"Yes, but it pays better," she said with a grin.

I grinned back. "That it does. The security on Carpenter's place is garbage. It would be easy to murder him in his bed. Why are people with that much money so cheap?"

"Greedy. Don't get greedy, Libby. All you have to do is look at your father. He could have walked away from his last job. He told me he knew he should walk away, but he got greedy."

She had probably told me that a thousand times. So had he. It was the most parental thing either of them ever did.

I left through the kitchen and swiped something to eat on my way out. The quality of the food Mom served was a lot better than I could find in the markets, low on toxic chemicals, heavy metals, and radiation. She had good connections.

Of course, the fact that I had the money to shop for fresh food in the markets spoke to my privileged place in society. Crime paid very well. Many people had never tasted a crisp, fresh apple.

A girl walking around alone at night wasn't safe, although I did it a lot. I changed back to my real form, but blurred into the shadows. I grabbed my motorcycle and rode through the business district, on through the entertainment district, and west into an upscale residential part of town. It was after midnight, but Dad's house was on my way home, and his light was on. I pressed my hand against the security pad, set my eye to the retinal scan, and keyed in the password. After a voice scan, the door opened and I let myself into the foyer.

"Dad? Are you awake?"

"Libby! Sure, I'm awake. Come on in." He came into sight, his power chair hovering over the floor. His house was customized and tailored to that chair. No rugs or carpet, no walls separating rooms, just a wide-open space past the foyer. One side of the wide staircase was a ramp. "You're out late. What's going on? Drink? Something to eat?"

"I'll take some fruit juice if you have it," I said. Like Mom, he had connections, plus he was fairly wealthy from his time as a corporate executive and his back-alley businesses. He had fallen six years before, while pulling a side job. The three-story drop left him a paraplegic and ended both of his careers.

If you saw me and Mom walking down the street, you'd never guess we were related. I looked even less like Dad. He was built like a fireplug and didn't fit anyone's stereotype of either an assassin or a cat burglar. Even before his accident, he was only five-foot-five, but carried a two hundred twenty pounds of solid muscle, compared to my slender six-foot-two. He had dark brown hair and his face often reminded people of a hound, with a large nose and heavy jowls.

I pulled the jewelry out of my bag and laid it on the table while he poured me a glass of juice. He came over and handed it to me, then whistled.

"Oh, my. You've been naughty, haven't you?" He picked up the emerald necklace. "Such a pity. Far too recognizable to leave intact. It will have to be broken up." He lifted his eyes to mine. "How did you stumble across this?"

"Stumble is right," I said. "I did a B and E to plant a cyber bug, and this was in the bedroom safe."

My dad, Jason Bouchard, was the former Chief of Security with MegaTech Corporation. He taught me martial arts, weapons, wall climbing, and how to crack a safe. He'd retired six years earlier, but he still had his contacts. Sometimes he brokered contracts for me and fenced anything I might need to sell.

"Do you mind my asking who the mark was?" he asked.

"Kahlil Carpenter."

He lifted an eyebrow. "Yes, it definitely needs to be broken up and probably sold on a different continent. I'll do some research to find where he bought it." He sorted through the other pieces—rings, earrings, bracelets, necklaces—mostly diamonds, but a couple of nice rubies. "The rest of this shouldn't be too difficult."

He fixed me with his patented you've-disappointed-me expression and held up the emerald necklace. "Why did you take it? Surely you could see how difficult it would be to move."

"Because it's so incredible. How many times in your life do you have a chance at something like that?"

He hadn't put the necklace down, stroking it, letting it slide through his fingers.

"Well, that's true. I probably wouldn't have passed it up, either. I hope you don't expect a quick payoff."

I shook my head. "I already got paid for the B and E. This is all gravy."

"Good. Come here." He had unclasped the necklace and was holding the ends apart. I walked over to him and crouched. He put his arms around my neck, and the weight of the necklace fell on my breastbone. "There," he said as he finished clasping it. "Stand up and turn around. Ohhh, yes. My God, Libby. It's too bad you can't keep it."

I walked into the foyer and scrutinized myself in the mirror. The necklace was large, but I was very tall. The white gold and emeralds were stunning against my black turtleneck. And if I wore it anywhere in public, Carpenter would bury me. I took it off and carried it back to the table.

"I don't need twenty million around my neck," I told him. "I might as well paint a target on my shirt."

CHAPTER 2

I didn't have any food in the house, or at least any substantial food, so after snacking all day I went out to dinner. I'm usually a jeans-and-a-t-shirt kind of girl, but I felt like eating at a nice restaurant to celebrate the successful job the previous night. I dressed up a bit, a black waist-length jacket over a red shirt and tight black stovepipe pants. I even brushed my hair out and put on some jewelry and high heels.

I was in a bit of a mood, some indefinable itch going on, and after dinner, I wandered down to The Pinnacle, the biggest, sweatiest, hippest dance club in town. The crowd was usually young corporate types and corporate scions, with a sprinkling of hot-chick gold diggers and wannabes. I always thought of myself as being in the "wannabe a hot chick" category.

I really fit in better in the mutant bars where looks and impressing people weren't that important. Sometimes beauty wasn't even skin deep. There was nothing like going home with a handsome mutie and discovering he was covered with scales except for his face and palms. Or he grew fur and acted like a wolf when the moon was full. Or he liked to suck a little blood with his sex.

My mutations weren't visible, or revolting, but there was a difference in attitude in the mutie places. A harder edge, and I was really not a soft girl, though I cleaned up pretty good.

I usually went to The Pinnacle, though, because my two best friends worked there. I walked in and realized how early I was. The band hadn't set up yet, and the club was three-quarters empty. I could even get a table by the stage if I wanted to.

"You're a bit earlier than usual," Paul Renard said

when I leaned against the bar.

I shrugged. "Just thought I'd drop by after breakfast and see how you're doing."

He laughed. "You need a hangover cure?"

"Nope. Cold sober last night. I was working."

For public consumption, I was a security consultant. I actually got quite a bit of work, and if I made the effort, could probably make a good living at it. But I could work my ass off for two months or more to earn what I made off that job the night before—not counting the jewelry.

"Nellie's singing tonight, isn't she?" I asked.

"Yeah, Blues Revival is playing. Drink?"

"Sure," I said. "Glass of white wine." He gave me a dubious look. "I'm starting off slow, okay? You're the one who said it was early."

"Real wine, or chemicals?" he asked, even though he should have known the answer.

"There's a difference? Wine, please. Hold the petroleum by-products." I knew I should be careful or I'd wake up in Paul's apartment in the club's basement. That was usually what happened when I got too drunk. Unfortunately, I fell into the only sexual category Paul didn't embrace—normal female. Pity, because he was very nice to look at.

I hung around and bothered him for a while, then bothered some of the other staff and regulars. That itch was getting worse, but I couldn't figure out what it was. To my knowledge, I wasn't precognizant, or at least I never had been before. In my business, it would have been helpful.

The band members filtered in and began setting up. Blues Revival played old-fashioned blues, R and B, and jazz, music from before the wars. They had a

13

recording contract and their videos were on the infonet. There was even talk about a European tour in the near future.

Nellie showed up with her sugar daddy, Richard O'Malley. Richard was a vice president with Entertaincorp, the corporation that owned The Pinnacle and Blues Revival's recording contract. Richard also owned Nellie's apartment and Nellie's time whenever he wanted it. She told me his wife and kids lived north of the city in a secure corporate compound. I hadn't robbed any homes in that particular compound, but I knew the type of place—trophy wives and a social life centered around the country club, the kids enrolled in university preparatory schools. No one ever met or associated with anyone who wasn't owned—body and soul—by the corporations.

Richard and I didn't get along very well. An educated independent, disparagingly referred to as an indie, seemed to unnerve him. I was one of the rare people who could have a corporate lifestyle and its security, but spurned it. In his world, you were either kissing the ass of the person above you on the corporate ladder, or fighting off the people who were kissing your ass. He couldn't comprehend someone with a grappling hook who just did whatever the hell she wanted.

From Nellie's point of view, her relationship with O'Malley was a business transaction. Beauty was a tradeable commodity, and those born below the top levels of society didn't start with much. Without her talent and looks, the best Nellie could have hoped for in life was a job as Richard's housemaid.

He stayed through about half of the band's first set, sitting in a mezzanine box next to the stage. The rapt expression on his face as he watched her sing told me that his feelings for her might go a little deeper than business. I filed that thought away, not knowing if it might ever have any value.

Nellie did have a spectacular voice—strong, sweet, and warm, with a smoky quality perfect for jazz and the blues. Nellie was also beautiful, petite and curvy, with long black hair and skin so smooth it always reminded me of buttered chocolate. She didn't need makeup, but she usually did her eyes and lips. Sometimes I couldn't contain myself and I'd reach out and stroke her skin with my fingertips, marveling at how smooth it was. I startled her the first time I'd done that, but afterwards she just smiled. She'd sailed through her teenage years without a single zit, and I'd been so envious.

When the band took its first break, she came to my table and sat down.

"You're sounding good tonight," I said. She always sounded good. "I brought you a present." I held out a pair of diamond studs. The earrings and their stones were unmarked and unidentifiable.

Nellie took them, held one up to the light, then turned wide eyes toward me. "These are real!"

"Of course they're real."

She shook her head. "Libby, the stones are huge!"

"Only a carat each. I wanted you to have them." I handed her an envelope I pulled from my bag. "This is for Miz Rollins. Will you give it to her for me?"

I received a suspicious scowl, and then she peeked inside the envelope. "How much is on that card?"

"Ten thousand."

"Oh, good God, Libby—" she started, but I put my fingers on her lips.

"I had a good month," I said. "What am I

supposed to do with it? Invest it in some corporate bank? They already have enough money."

Amanda Rollins ran a sort of orphanage for mutant children. Mutations that were disfiguring, and often somewhat disabling. Her heart was far larger than her wallet or her common sense.

Nellie shook her head and took a deep breath. "You can't give away everything you earn, Libby. You never know when your situation might change. You have to look to the future, girl."

"I'll worry about me," I said. "I've never missed a meal in my life. Corporate brat, remember?"

She sputtered. "Lilith's isn't a corporation. It could disappear tomorrow."

I chuckled. "So could Margrave Corp." Khalil Carpenter was CEO of Margrave, one of the top ten employers in the city.

She froze with her mouth open as what I said filtered through to her. Leaning forward and dropping her voice, she asked, "What have you heard?"

"I wouldn't buy stock in Margrave."

A sly expression crossed her face. "Maybe I should short it?" Everyone in the lower classes had dreams of making a killing in the stock market.

"I wouldn't do that either," I told her. "Nellie, stay away from the corps. They aren't ever going to do anything good for people like us. You want to invest in something, save your money and someday we'll buy an apartment building together." Real estate had done okay for my dad.

She reluctantly nodded. "I know. I just worry sometimes. Remember Galina? Real pretty blonde with the big boobs?"

"Yeah?"

"She got turned out of her apartment last week. Man had a younger girl in there as soon as the cleaning crew was done. What would I do if Richard gets tired of me?"

"You're more than a pair of big boobs," I said.

Nellie glanced down at her chest. "I certainly hope so."

We both laughed.

"You're talented," I said. "You can sing, you write songs, and that won't go away when you get old. Save your money. We'll buy a place. Okay?"

She nodded. "Gotta go sing. You gonna stick around?"

"Yeah. I assume O'Malley went home to the wife?"

"Yeah."

"I planned on walking you home."

She gave me a thousand-watt smile. "I'd like that."

⊕|⊕|⊕

The lead story in the following morning's newscast concerned a new class of drugs flooding the Toronto area. The same drugs were appearing in Buffalo, Chicago, Detroit, and Montreal. When drugs killed people in the poor areas of town, no one cared. But this seemed to be popular with prep school teens and university students. In other words, the children of the corporate elite.

Something about the story sounded off, so I did some checking online. Nothing in Atlanta or Portland or Edmonton. Nothing in Europe. A couple of news stories in Ottawa and one in Dallas. If I plotted the stories on a map, everything centered on Toronto.

That afternoon I got a call from Dad. "I've got a

job for you," he said. Since we were talking on the phone, I assumed it was a legitimate job. "Do you have a couple of weeks?"

"Sure. Who's it for?"

"Maya Wellington. Her husband is Simon Wellington of Hudson Bay Exploration. She wants a security assessment and upgrade on their estate." He chuckled. "They live about a half-mile from Khalil Carpenter."

I pulled my motorcycle out of the garage, checked the charge and rode out to the Wellington estate.

I knew from my online research that their estate covered twice as much area as Carpenter's. I arrived an hour before my appointment so I could look around. I blurred my form to blend in and checked the place from the outside. Twelve-foot walls with concertina wire, lots of cameras, and pressure plates outside the walls. Lights all over the place. Wellington had spent the money Carpenter hadn't, and the security appeared pretty solid.

After a thorough appraisal, I presented my credentials to the guards at the gate, and an escort took me to the cute little fifty-room bungalow.

The place swarmed with servants. When you were the head of a gold-mining and petroleum company you could afford a lavish lifestyle.

Maya Wellington met me and showed me around the house. Tastefully but casually dressed, Maya was the ultimate corporate wife. Beautiful, charming, and witty. She immediately made me comfortable and gave me the impression of intelligence and competence.

After the quickie tour, she called her head of security, Aaron Fitzgerald, and he took me around the grounds. When we finished, I thanked him and said

I'd be back the next morning to start evaluating things in depth.

I spent the next week checking out the systems, crawling along the walls, testing for vulnerabilities. I came out at night, blended into the shadows and watched the guards. When I finished my report, I asked for a meeting with Mrs. Wellington.

"I'm a little puzzled as to why you asked me to come out here," I started. "Your equipment is state of the art and appears to be newly upgraded. Mr. Fitzgerald is very professional and his staff is well-trained and disciplined. I'll run my findings past Mr. Bouchard in case I missed something, but I don't think I have."

She nodded, then took a deep breath. "That's very good to know. What I'm really worried about is whether someone can get out."

I mulled that over, then cautiously asked, "And who are you trying to keep in?" Slavery was banned under all international trade agreements, but some of the corporate execs considered themselves above societal norms.

"My children."

I must have reacted in some noticeable way because she nodded. "Yes, I know how that sounds. My son Mark, primarily, but Susan also. They're twins, you see. I'm afraid they've started experimenting with drugs. I don't know if you've heard, but there's a new drug called luvdaze that's causing a lot of overdoses."

"I've heard of it. One of the newscasts said it was popular among prep and university students."

"Unfortunately, yes. One of our vice presidents lost his daughter last week. When we found out Mark was using it, we grounded him and upgraded the security. But he's still getting out, and we don't know how."

I thought about it, then said, "Mrs. Wellington, you pay me to think outside normal boundaries. What I'm about to say isn't meant to be offensive or judgmental."

She cocked her head a bit to the side. "Go on."

"Is it possible that Mark has a mutation? Even the best of families aren't immune."

"But, what kind of mutation could get him out through the security system?"

I took a deep breath. "Among other things, some people have shown the ability to disrupt electrical devices. Some psychic abilities might allow a person to walk out the front gate without being noticed. It wouldn't have to be Mark, either. It could be Susan."

Wellington stared off into space for well over a minute, then bent down and took off her shoes. I had noticed she had very big feet, but now I saw why. Her toes were very long with webbing between them. Like flippers.

"You're correct, Miss Nelson. Even the best families aren't immune. Susan and Mark inherited my feet." She chuckled. "We're all excellent swimmers." She put her shoes back on. "But if that's the case, how do we figure out what it is, and more importantly, how to stop him? Susan has some common sense, but Mark has always seemed to think he's invulnerable."

"How old are they?"

"Seventeen."

Yeah, kids that age were pretty stupid.

"Have you ever experimented with drugs?" Wellington asked me.

"No, I didn't, but I knew kids who did. Both of my

parents worked in corporate security, and they made it very clear what kinds of behavior they wouldn't forgive."

When Dad said he'd drop me off a cliff, I wasn't inclined to test if he was serious. Even as a paraplegic, he was still the most intimidating man I'd ever met.

"Maybe we should have done a better job of that, but Simon has always indulged Mark."

"Mrs. Wellington, I can try to catch him sneaking out, but the charges will be by the hour, and there's no guarantee of success. Even if I do succeed, it may take a week or more."

She gave a dismissive wave of her hand. "Obviously money isn't a problem. What do you need from me?"

"Free run of your house and grounds. Passwords so I can get in and out. You know that I'm bonded up to ten million for any losses."

She chuckled. "I went to school with your mother. I contacted her for this and she recommended Mr. Bouchard. I was rather surprised when he offered you for the job. I would have thought Lettie might have recommended you."

"Mom's specialty is cyber security. She defers to him for physical security. They both trained me, and I take referrals from both of them."

"I'll tell Fitzgerald to provide what you need."

And just like that, I had the keys to one of the richest castles in Canada. Too bad I couldn't do anything with them.

⊕|⊕|⊕

The first two nights I watched from outside the

Wellington's wall, I didn't see anything. When I checked with Mrs. Wellington the following mornings, I discovered her children were home. The third night, I saw a car stop around the corner, turn out its lights and wait.

I waited, too.

About twenty minutes later, Mark and Susan came down the road from the direction of the front gate. It didn't take a genius to figure out the next step. I got my motorcycle and followed them out to the main highway.

They drove into Toronto and straight to the entertainment district near the lake. Pulling up in front of a club called the Drop Inn, they got out, and the valet took the car. Mark, Susan and the driver, another girl about their age or a little older, went into the club. Since the job paid expenses, I let the valet take my motorcycle, too.

The crowd seemed a little young to me, and drugs of various types were exchanging hands like germs in a kindergarten. The haze from the weed smoke was so bad that I kept my mask on. Most of the customers and the staff took theirs off. I guessed they liked the free high.

I tried to keep an eye on Mark more than on the others. The driver was obviously his girlfriend, and just as obviously, the source of the drugs. Maya Wellington was correct in her concerns. I didn't see Susan use anything harder than weed. Mark and his girlfriend snorted what I assumed was either coke or meth, then a while later they each took a shot from a jet injector.

Observing them and some of the other kids, I became convinced the jet injectors contained the luvdaze everyone was worried about. By midnight, people were passing out all over the place. The bouncers didn't seem to care, and it occurred to me that while the majority of the customers were corporate kids, the club wasn't corporate.

Susan pulled her brother and their friend outside around two o'clock, and when the valet brought the car, she got behind the wheel. I hoped she would let the computer drive them home.

⊕⊕⊕

My next step was to watch from inside the compound the following night. I called Fitzgerald and cleared my plan with him. My personal jet pack lifted me over the Wellington's wall and carried me beyond the perimeter detectors. The device was pricey, but I hadn't paid for it. I'd picked it up as kind of a bonus on another job where the security was worse than Carpenter's.

A large tree had a clear line of sight to both the house and the front gate. I climbed it with my night-vision binoculars and found a comfortable place on a large limb. I waited all night but nothing happened.

Around midnight, bored out of my mind, I pulled out my tablet and did some more research on luvdaze. A couple of articles convinced me it was bad stuff. They also told me why Mark wasn't trying to sneak out every night.

The effects of luvdaze started with feelings of euphoria and mild hallucinations that crested into a feeling of being one with the world, powerful and invulnerable. At that point in the trip, users became sexually hyperactive. All of this lasted about twelve hours. The following phase involved a tailing off, lassitude, and finally, sleep for another twelve hours.

Even the most hardcore addicts only took it every three days. They didn't have the energy to do it more often.

Other than the drug taking over a person's life, the major issue was that over time the addict developed a tolerance. Unfortunately not a physical tolerance, but a perceived tolerance. When the drug didn't deliver the kick it used to and the feelings of power weren't as great, the user tended to take more. Only, a little more was a death sentence. The brainstem seized and the person stopped breathing.

The drug was usually sold on the streets as a single dosage jet injector. If the dealer loaded too much in the devices, a mass overdose might occur, which had happened in Chicago a couple of weeks before.

I climbed down out of my tree and went home.

Two nights later, I was back in the tree. A little after dark, Mark and Susan came out of a door on the side of the house. Checking the house plan on my tablet, I found it was the door from the kitchen to the garbage bins. They circled around the house, through the rose garden and a small orchard onto the lawn.

The orchard blocked them from being seen from the house windows, and they nonchalantly walked up to the main gate. Mark pulled an envelope from his pocket and handed it to the guards on duty, who opened the gate.

Ah, the magic of money. Occam's razor. The simplest solution was the most likely. I'd been thinking like a thief, envisioning technology, mutations, and elaborate schemes, not like a rich, overly-entitled teen.

I pulled out my phone and called Fitzgerald. As I climbed down from the tree and prepared to hop back over the wall, I saw a van with Fitzgerald and other security guards pull out from the back of the house and head down the drive to the main gate. It stopped there and I saw someone get out. Then the gate opened and the van drove on. When I drove out of the subdivision, I saw Mark's girlfriend's car and the security van stopped by the side of the road, surrounded by Fitzgerald's security men.

I spoke with both Fitzgerald and Mrs. Wellington the next day and transmitted my invoice.

CHAPTER 3

The band was rocking it at The Pinnacle when I heard, "Wanna dance?"

I glanced up, and then up a little more. He was tall, with nice shoulders, and a nice smile.

"Sure." I stood, watching his face as I rose to my full six feet two inches, plus the heels I was wearing. A lot of men want women shorter than they are. My eyes passed his, and then his followed mine up. I figured if I had been barefoot, we would've been about the same height. His smile didn't falter, and he reached for my hand. Okay! I smiled back.

We sized each other up as we danced. I liked what I saw. Broad shoulders, broad chest, muscular arms. Buzz haircut. A hint of tattoo peeking out from his sleeves and collar. Gold hoop in one ear.

We danced to a couple more songs, then he bought me a drink.

"I'm Ron," he said as he handed me a glass with something orangish in it.

"Libby."

"You're hot."

"Thanks." I motioned toward the stage. "I'm going home with her tonight."

He puckered his lips, then took a drink. "You always swing that way?"

"I swing all sorts of ways. Mostly I don't swing at all. I'm kinda picky and I don't get in a hurry."

To my surprise, he smiled. "Nothing wrong with that." He toasted me with his glass, then took another drink. "You come here a lot?"

"Fairly regular."

"I'll see ya again, then," Ron said and wandered off into the crowd. A couple of minutes later I saw him dancing with another woman. Good to know I didn't permanently crush his heart.

The orange thing tasted terrible, so I took it over to the bar and shoved it at Paul. "Give me a shot of whiskey. I need something to wash the taste of that out of my mouth."

Paul laughed. "I tried to tell him you wouldn't like it." He poured me a shot. "My treat," he said, leaning forward to hand me the drink. "See that guy down at the end of the bar? He asked if Elizabeth Nelson is here tonight."

I craned my neck to see the man Paul was talking about. He looked like a corporate type, dressed in a business suit. Even my mother didn't call me Elizabeth, but it was the name on my business card. "What did you tell him?"

"That I hadn't seen you yet. Says his name is Sayd Agha."

"Any hint as to what he wants?"

Paul shook his head.

I walked down the bar. "Mr. Agha? I'm Elizabeth Nelson. I understand you were asking for me."

He slid off the bar stool and stood. "Ah, Miss Nelson. Yes, I would like to discuss some business with you." He had to crane his neck up to talk to me and it seemed to bother him.

I handed him my business card. "Normally, people either send me an email or vmail. We can discuss your business tomorrow." Rather than walk away, I hesitated, waiting to see what he would do. Expecting me at The Pinnacle was a curious choice since I had no official connection to the place. The idea that he had followed me there seeped through my alcohol-soaked brain.

"I hoped we might talk tonight," he said, reaching out and taking my elbow. "Perhaps we could just go outside where it's quieter." I tried to shake him off, and he tightened his grip. "I think we need to talk now, Miss Nelson."

"Perhaps we could go into the women's washroom so I can torture you until you tell me what this is about," I suggested. I stared in his eyes, but he wasn't sufficiently shocked at what I'd said. A man who nonchalantly considered torture a standard topic of conversation? Not good.

"Look down," I said. He glanced down at the knife I held against his abdomen. "Let go of me." He did. "Very good. Now, turn around and face the bar. And if you think you might be faster than I am, consider if you'd bet your life on it."

Agha made a good decision and turned around. I took a small electroshock box from my purse, put it against the back of his neck and gave him three million volts. His shaking-dance reaction attracted Paul's attention, and he rushed around the end of the bar to catch my victim before he fell.

"Do you have a room where we can take him?" I asked. "Or do I have to drag him all the way to the basement?"

"Are you going to kill him?" Paul asked. Did I mention that Paul had known me for a very long time?

"Not until I find out how many friends he has outside. I have no idea what's going on."

Paul turned away and told another bartender to cover for him. He spoke into a mic clipped to his collar, then turned back to me.

"I called for a couple of bouncers to help us."

We both scanned the room, trying to see if anyone was taking an interest in our activities. It didn't appear anyone was paying attention. I pulled out my phone and called my dad.

"Hey, does the name Sayd Agha ring a bell?" I asked when Dad answered.

"Can't say that it does. Why?"

"He just tried to lure me outside a club to talk business. I told him to call the office tomorrow, and he tried to get insistent."

"Don't go with him!"

I chuckled. "I didn't. I can't figure out why he's interested in me, so I thought maybe you'd run over his pet frog or something."

"Send me his picture."

Two bouncers, Tom and Ramon, showed up and carried Agha down the stairs to the basement. I thought we were going to Paul's apartment, but they surprised me. We ended up in a laundry room. Paul brought a chair, and one of the bouncers produced a rope. They were very efficient in tying my new friend to the chair.

"Looks like you boys have done this before," I commented.

Tom winked at me.

"If he followed me here, his friends may know Nellie is a friend of mine," I said.

Ramon's grin turned into a scowl. "Anyone touch Nellie has a death wish." I didn't think he was speaking metaphorically. He nodded to Tom, who headed toward the stairs.

"Do you need me?" Paul asked. When I shook my head, he also left, but Ramon stayed.

"You here to protect me or him?" I asked.

"I don't know him, and he ain't near as pretty as you are. You're Paul's friend." He stepped back and leaned against a washing machine.

My phone rang. "Dad?"

"His name is Adnan Erdowan," Dad said. "He's Turkish, but he's been living here for about ten years. He works for a Russian electronics corporation."

"That's nice. By here, do you mean Toronto or North America?"

"North America. He's based in Dallas, but airline records show he's been shuttling back and forth from Dallas to Toronto monthly for the past year."

"Any idea why he's after me?"

"None. I've never dealt with that company, one way or the other." Then he gave me his version of fatherly advice. "Libby, don't take any chances and don't leave any witnesses."

I hung up and told the bouncer, "Maybe you should take a look outside and see if anyone's waiting for him."

"Already have people doing that."

"Oh. Are you squeamish?"

"Not particularly."

I shoved the little box into the Turk's groin and triggered it. He screamed—long, loud, and raw. The bouncer paled. I decided he lied when he said he wasn't squeamish. Men are like that—always trying to put on a strong front.

I grabbed Adnan's hair and said into his ear. "Adnan Erdowan. You lied to me. You either tried to kidnap me or you planned to kill me. If you hope to see another sunrise, you'd better start talking."

30

He glared at me but stayed silent.

"Can you help me position him over the drain?" I asked the bouncer. "Might as well keep the cleanup to a minimum." I took off my jacket and started unbuttoning my shirt.

"What are you doing?" Ramon asked.

"I don't want to get blood on my clothes." I'm not sure if either he or Erdowan believed me at first, but they certainly paid more attention when I pulled off my top and then unfastened my pants. I folded my clothes and put them up on a shelf, then grabbed Adnan by the hair and pulled the chair over backward. His head bounced off the floor with a sound like a dropped melon. The bouncer stared at the knife I pulled from a sheath in my bra.

I dragged Adnan by the hair to the drain in the floor and told Ramon, "You can go. I really don't want any witnesses."

I leaned down and drew the tip of the knife lightly across Adnan's throat. He froze, his eyes very wide, as I showed him a drop of his blood running down the blade. I grinned at him and said, "Last chance."

He started babbling. Unfortunately, it was in Turkish. When I finally convinced him to speak English, we learned that three of his friends were waiting outside in a car. He didn't know why they were ordered to drug me, kidnap me, and take me to their boss. Yes, this was corporate business. Interestingly, they didn't know where I lived. They hadn't followed me, but they were told to find me at The Pinnacle.

Very sloppy. Dad would have grounded me for a month if I moved on a target with so little information. Well, back when he still had the authority to ground me. But still, very sloppy.

After I got everything Adnan knew, I retrieved a jet injector from my purse and gave Adnan a shot in the neck.

"Dead?" the bouncer asked.

"Naw, just sleeping. Do you think you could dump him in the garbage out back for me?"

"Sure." He seemed relieved that he didn't have to deal with a corpse.

Ramon hustled over and untied our captive while I got dressed. When I finished, I walked over, bent down, grabbed his chin, and kissed him full on the lips with a lot of tongue. He didn't fight back. Men are so easy.

"Thank you, Ramon," I said with a smile, then left and went upstairs.

I stopped by the bar and told Paul how to identify Adnan's friends, then ducked out of the club's back door.

⊕|⊕|⊕

I had always been inquisitive. Mom and Dad thought I was too inquisitive, but I got it from them. An unsolved puzzle would drive both of them crazy.

Maybe that was why their on-off-on-off relationship had lasted so long. I used to think it was me, which is a good thing for a kid to think. A kid should feel as though her parents think she's important. Especially if she's the result of a drunken one-night stand between two people of different social classes who are twenty years apart in age.

But the last few years, I'd come to the conclusion that their attraction to each other was another puzzle thing. They drove each other crazy, couldn't figure out what made the other one tick, and couldn't figure out why they couldn't stay away from each other. I was the excuse they used for keeping in touch. I had no idea how they explained to themselves why they kept sleeping with each other. Their whole relationship was weird. My entire family dynamic was weird.

So, I blamed my DNA for not walking out of The Pinnacle and putting a lot of distance between me and the Russian corporate thugs in the parking lot. Instead, I grabbed a small can from my purse and snuck around the side of the building. Their car didn't stand out in a parking lot filled by corporate type cars. On the other hand, it was the only one with three men sitting inside.

Crouching low, I crept up behind them without being noticed. Two men in the front and one in the back. None of them wore their filter masks. Using the mutation inherited from my mother to short out the car's electrical system, including the locks, I jerked the backdoor open and sprayed the men inside, then slammed the door shut.

One of the club's bouncers strolled over and peered into the window. "Nasty stuff," he commented, glancing up at me. "What is it?"

"A knockout gas." I held up the can to show him. "I'm sure Entertaincorp security can buy it. All the leading security infonet sites carry it."

The guy in the backseat tried to open the car's door, but I kicked it back shut. He swayed and then fell over.

We waited another five minutes, then opened the doors and let the car air out. I dragged the men out of the car one by one, searched them, and gave them a dose of the jet injector I'd given Adnan. When I finished, I stripped them all to the skin, threw their clothes in the car and lit it on fire.

"Holy shit!" the bouncer yelled. "You are one radical bitch!"

I gave him a smile that caused him to back up a couple of steps. "Yes, I am. I really don't like people fucking with me. Feel free to pass that advice along."

I went back into the club, bought a drink, and listened to Nellie sing.

⊕|⊕|⊕

Research on Elektronika Upravlyaet—translated as Electronics Controls, the Russian corporation my dad identified—didn't turn up any rationale as to why they took a run at me. The corporation was a mid-level player on the international scene, primarily manufacturing industrial control equipment for factories and oil refineries.

I even hacked into their systems and didn't find anything I considered a clue. They had their own security apparatus, of course, but they wouldn't care for my opinion of their cyber security. It appeared as though they used their own people for assassinations and dirty tricks. Sloppy to leave evidence of that online. Adnan and his buddies were pretty sloppy, too, evidently in keeping with the corporate culture.

I was extra careful for a couple of weeks, but when nothing unusual happened, I relaxed into my normal state of rabid paranoia and sort of forgot about Adnan and his friends.

Then one day, Dad called and asked me to drop by. I briefly wondered if he might have fenced some of Carpenter's jewelry but didn't ask. We never discussed business except in person.

"I received an inquiry for a job," Dad said after we sat down and shared some cookies and lemonade. The little crook at the corner of his mouth and the sparkle in his eyes gave me warning of a surprise coming. "It's a hit on Nikolai Sholokhov, Elektronika Upravlyaet's North American sales director. Adnan Erdowan's boss."

I barked out a startled laugh.

"The best part, though, is the client," he continued.

I held my breath because he almost never told me who contracted my services. He trained me not to be curious about that.

"The client is Andrei Saakashvili, who is Sholokhov's boss."

He watched me closely, waiting for me to put it all together. I had to be careful. If I came to the wrong conclusion, he'd shred me. If I took too long reaching the correct conclusion, he'd shred me. He didn't give jobs to stupid assassins, and I wasn't the only tool in his box.

"One explanation might be that Saakashvili found out Sholokhov put a hit on him," I said. "Sholokhov couldn't use Electronika's own men on an internecine hit, so he went looking elsewhere. No idea how he got my name. Their approach certainly wasn't very businesslike."

I tried to be cool while I waited for Dad's decision. Have another cookie, Libby. Take a drink of lemonade. Try to control your urge to scream at your father.

"That's the same line of reasoning I followed," he said, "but it still doesn't feel right."

That was as close to a "well done" as I ever got

from him.

"Standard fee?" I asked.

"Twenty-five percent bonus if it looks like an accident. They're brothers-in-law."

⊕⊕⊕

CHAPTER 4

The definition of an accident is rather broad. Falling off a cliff is an accident, being pushed isn't. A car wreck is an accident, a car wreck because the brake lines were cut isn't. A heart attack is an accident, poison that stops the heart isn't. Insurance companies tend to define an accident very narrowly. They have no sense of humor when it comes to paying claims.

Dad gave me a dossier on the target, which was only a starting point. I committed it all to memory and reviewed everything available online. Since I'd cracked Elektronika's network already, I was ahead of my normal timeframe. Three days later, I packed my kit and headed for the airport.

Elektronika's regional headquarters was in Dallas, a center of the North American petroleum business even before the oceans rose and the missiles fell. I had been in Dallas before, but not in the summer. I stepped off the plane, and the heat and humidity hit me like a club. I knew I was on the edge of the Great Southwestern Desert, but knowing and experiencing are often very different things.

Luckily, the majority of the metropolis was either inside or underground, and air-conditioned. The old aboveground city with its skyscrapers was visible in the distance, now inhabited by rats, muties, and the desperately poor.

One thing I did like about Dallas, since so much of it was covered, was that I didn't need to wear my filter mask all the time. The outside air was foul, but I was rarely out in it.

The monorail took me to my hotel, where I tapped into Elektronika's network, and then into Sholokhov's

37

calendar and private files. Building a catalogue of the target's movements and habits would be the truly boring part of the job.

After a week, I started wondering if the accident premium was worth the effort. Sholokhov never went anywhere alone, except to visit Maria, his mistress. Even then, two bodyguards accompanied him and waited for him. Arranging an accident was going to be difficult. One thing Dad had drummed into me—collateral damage was unprofessional.

Normally, the two ways to take out an unapproachable target were poison or a long-range rifle. Since I had no way of observing the inside of Sholokhov's home or business, I would have to poison the food going in. Someone else would also eat the food, so collateral damage was inevitable. Saakashvili certainly wouldn't pay a premium if I killed his sister. Hurting the mistress was something I didn't even consider. How would I feel if someone killed Nellie in an attempt on O'Malley? A rifle bullet was difficult to pass off as an accident, so I pushed that off as a last resort.

I thought about how I might be able to use my mutations at the mistress's apartment. The place was full of cameras and I watched Maria and Sholokhov when he went to visit.

Early on, I considered kidnapping the mistress and taking her place. That wouldn't gain me very much. I still had to figure out what kind of accident Sholokhov could have.

I decided to spend a day following the mistress around, thinking a change in her routine might produce a brilliant idea. At the very least, I would need to know what she sounded like and what her mannerisms were if I did decide to take her place.

Maria Lopez, Sholokhov's mistress, approached shopping the way a general approached a battle. In a little more than two hours before she stopped for lunch, she tallied up at least twenty grand. If Sholokhov let her do that on a regular basis, I had to wonder if the true source of the contract to kill him might be his wife.

Speaking of the wife, Maria resembled a younger version. Medium height, busty, with long dark-brown hair, brown eyes, and an olive complexion. Actually, when I got the chance to see Maria close up, she was a dead ringer for Sholokhov's oldest daughter. I shied away from that thought.

Lunch was excellent. For those prices, anything less than outstanding would have been a cause for complaint. I wandered into the restaurant about five minutes after Maria did and took a table fifteen feet away from her. Close enough that I could read the label on the wine she ordered and match it to a two-hundred-credit price on the menu. I contented myself with a twenty-credit bottle of mineral water.

A friend of hers joined her, so I got to see more of how she interacted with people, how she laughed, how snide she was about the waitress. I didn't like her or her friend much after that.

They spent two hours eating lunch, and getting fairly drunk. Then the two of them evidently decided they needed new shoes and purses. A truckload of shoes and purses. Then they spent a couple of hours shopping for lingerie. Afterward, they went to dinner at a place a decimal point more upscale than the bistro where they had lunch. I wasn't dressed for that, but I had a few patterns stored away in my mind.

I morphed into a fifty-year-old woman with more money than God. The pearls alone could have bought the restaurant if they were real.

"No, I don't have a reservation, young man. Don't you know who I am?" They gave me a great table next to a window where I could watch the sunset.

I perused the menu and decided I should have grabbed a burger and waited for them outside. This type of contract didn't come with expenses covered. But as long as I was emptying the bank account, I decided to go all out and ordered a lobster. I had never eaten one, or even seen one, but I'd heard of them and knew they were supposed to be a delicacy. I figured for that kind of money, it should be relatively free of toxins and radiation.

It was a bit of a shock when the waiter delivered a huge platter of bug. He was nice and explained that it only looked like a bug. He showed me how to eat it, and it tasted wonderful. Someday I might try it again.

Maria and her friend dropped a month's income for a corporate mid-level manager. I'd been around some pretty obnoxious rich corporate types, but I'd never seen anyone spend money the way they did. The fanciest wine and champagne, caviar and a custom-made dessert. I consoled myself with the thought that the caviar would probably glow if the lights went out.

I almost lost them after dinner when they called a taxi. I'd seen some old movies from before the wars where someone jumps in a taxi and says, "Follow that car!" Try that with a robotaxi. It just kept asking for my destination before it would move. I was tempted to short the damned thing out, but then it would never move again.

Instead, I got out and asked the doorman if he knew where the two young ladies ahead of me had gone. Twenty cred got me an answer. They were going to a club.

I changed forms in the taxi. I thought I'd looked pretty hot the night at The Pinnacle when that guy Ron hit on me, so I used the same clothing.

The club was definitely upscale. I had to flash corporate identification to get in, forged, of course. Keep the riff-raff out. I thought about Nellie's friend Galina and wondered how Maria would take it when Sholokhov found someone younger. Without his patronage, that corporate ID card would disappear along with the expense account.

The music was canned, and I sniggered when they played one of Nellie's songs. Only a few people were drinking beer, and that out of fancy goblets. Pretty pastel drinks with fruit and umbrellas seemed to be the norm. I ordered lemonade, and the bartender stuck an umbrella in it.

It took me a little while, but I figured out a lot of the people were doing some kind of drug. It wasn't as obvious as the Drop Inn, but then I spotted a woman and a man shoot themselves with little one-shot jet injectors. As the night wore on, they became increasingly amorous, like a number of other couples.

The women I was following were dancing and flirting. I knew from Sholokhov's calendar that he was out at the opera with his wife, and would be returning to his estate for the weekend afterward. Maria had time to herself, and from the looks of things, she planned to take advantage of it. Nellie and the other kept women I knew were as monogamous as their sugar daddies. I assumed it went with the territory.

I turned down a guy who asked me to dance. At the sound of my voice, a man a few feet in front of me spun around and stared at me. It was Adnan.

Two steps took me in reach of him, and I gathered him into a hug with my arms around his neck.

41

"It's so good to see you! Where have you been keeping yourself?" I gushed. No one around us could see the six-inch stainless steel hatpin I took from its sheath in my bra. "We really need to get together sometime soon and catch up!" I stuck the pin in his ear and pushed it into his brain. "Gotta go. Give me a call!"

I whirled and headed for the washroom, leaving him standing there, swaying slightly as if he had too much to drink. It takes some time for the body to realize the brain has been mortally wounded. In addition to the physical damage to his brainstem and temporal lobe, the hatpin was coated in a neurotoxin which started spreading through his system.

I passed the washroom and slipped out a side exit. Walking around to the back of the building, I let the clothing image go. A block away, I flagged down a robotaxi and had it take me to my hotel.

The club had cameras, just as there were cameras almost everywhere. When I checked in, I found one in my room. Correction. There was a camera in the shower. It developed a malfunction.

The worst part about running into Adnan was that I had to change identities. Of course, I had backups, but it was inconvenient to have to rearrange my identity. I transferred the credits in the account I'd been using to a Swiss bank, burned all of my identification, changed clothes, packed, and left. The hotel room was paid for another week. Maybe no one would check on me.

I shorted out the camera in the elevator and morphed into a form that was six inches shorter, with brown hair. A taxi took me to a hotel a couple of blocks away, then another taxi took me to a different hotel. I checked in there, morphed into a redhead, and caught a taxi to another hotel.

⊕|⊕|⊕

When I woke up in the morning, I had absolutely no idea where I was, though it was obviously a hotel room. It was sort of comforting. If I didn't know, maybe no one else did. Room service brought me breakfast and I logged into Elektronika's network. There wasn't any evidence online that Sholokhov knew Adnan was dead. Some of the security team did, though, and someone had ordered an autopsy. That meant they weren't sure how he died.

The security logs on Maria's apartment showed that she hadn't come home the night before. I hoped she had a good time.

I morphed into Maria and took the monorail to a stop near her apartment. Security wasn't a problem since I had already compromised Elektronika's main security controls. I thought it was interesting that Maria didn't have the authorization to reset the passwords to her own home. I wondered if she knew how many cameras it contained. Knowing about the cameras would be a good reason for not bringing a man home with her.

I also wondered if Sholokhov was the kind of man who would change the codes one day while she was out, leaving her on the street with only the clothes on her back. Some of the corporate execs were real bastards.

Inside, the first thing I did was turn off the camera in the bathroom. That would set off an alarm to Elektronika's security team if anyone noticed. Since I wasn't sure how closely they watched her, I needed to work fast.

I rerouted some of the bathroom's wiring and added an amperage booster to the circuit, then added a new switch in the camera. With that done, I reactivated the camera and left.

As I walked down the street to the monorail, a robotaxi drove by with Maria sitting inside. She had a bad case of bed head.

⊕⊕⊕

CHAPTER 5

With at least two days of waiting ahead of me, I turned tourist. Atlanta and Dallas were the two largest metropolises in the south and major destinations in the winter. Unfortunately, I was there in the summer, and outside temperatures ran from one hundred five degrees late at night to one hundred forty degrees in the afternoon. On the plus side, I was practically the only tourist in town.

I picked up some small gifts for my friends and visited the botanical gardens and the aquarium. It was both neat and depressing to see species of plants, animals and fish that were extinct except in such controlled environments. The really depressing exhibit, though, contained animals with extreme mutations.

Toronto was far enough north and inland that the climate changes weren't too severe, although I'd read that it used to snow there. Dallas had a whole museum devoted to the planetary holocaust. Governments had been slow to deal with pollution of the air, water, and soil. When the environment heated up, they didn't respond until the ice at the poles melted and the oceans rose enough to inundate the coastal cities.

At the same time, Northern Africa, the Middle East and the Indian subcontinent grew too hot for people to survive or grow food. The migration of hundreds of millions of people was met by a nuclear wall as the Europeans, Russians and Chinese tried to keep from being overrun. But the people they bombed had nukes, too.

Two hundred years later, we had barely recovered the level of technology that existed before the wars.

The world population was only a third of what it had been, and it was a struggle to feed us all. It reminded me of how lucky I was that my parents were rich. The corporations took care of the majority of the population, but even then, fresh fruit, vegetables, and meat were luxuries to all but the upper classes.

One of the museums had an outdoor exhibit. It might have been doable in the winter, but after five minutes, the heat drove me back inside.

At night, I hit a couple of clubs. Not the corporate ones, but those for the lower classes. I found one high-end mutie bar that was a riot. Great band, nice people, draft beer to die for, like the Pinnacle without the corporate snobs. The kind of place Toronto needed.

In one club, the open drug use was really blatant. The crowd was a little older than the Drop Inn, and a lot of people were using jet injectors to shoot up what I assumed was luvdaze. It really seemed to energize them, and the club practically turned into an orgy later in the evening. So not my scene.

⊕⊕⊕

Sholokhov came back into town after the weekend, and I started following him around again. His security personnel and arrangements continued as before, so it didn't seem that Adnan's death set off any alarms. Corporate life might pay well, but I found it rather boring. It seemed as though he did the same things day after day. The only break in his routine was Maria.

He didn't go to see her on Monday, instead spending the evening entertaining clients. But on Tuesday, he went to her place after dinner.

I tapped into Elektronika's network and accessed

46

the cameras in Maria's apartment. Watching the two of them go at it in her bedroom, I wondered if Sholokhov knew about all of the cameras. Maybe he was an exhibitionist and liked showing off to his security people. Maria was young and pretty and put on a show, but he was fifty-two and at least fifty pounds overweight. I would much rather have watched a vid, but needed to monitor the situation.

Along about midnight, he got up and went to the bathroom to take a shower. While he washed, I flipped the switch I had hidden in the camera.

He finished and stepped out of the shower, reaching out to grasp the metal bar anchored to the wall. As soon as he touched it, he froze and his body started shaking.

I switched off the current, then switched it back on for another thirty seconds, then off again. Two hundred twenty volts at four hundred milliamps sent Sholokhov's heart into tachycardia. He sank to the floor and turned a ghastly blue-gray. With a jerk, he stopped breathing.

Electrocution was one of the least common methods of murder. When it was used, it was almost always a crime of passion. Throwing a hair dryer into a bathtub wasn't the sort of thing you planned. A large electrical surge would kill immediately, but would also cause visible burns. My plan had been to induce a heart attack with amperage low enough that it didn't cause visible marks. It looked as though it worked, but I wouldn't know until Dad hit the client for the bonus.

As I packed and made my plane reservations, I wondered if Maria was smart enough to do the same.

She should throw everything worth selling in a bag and get the hell out the minute she found him.

⊕⊕⊕

I dropped by Dad's on my way home from the airport to let him know I was safe and that I'd completed the assignment. He had a pleasant surprise for me—proceeds from part of the Carpenter jewelry.

The next day was a typical Toronto summer day, cloudy with temperatures in the mid to upper nineties Fahrenheit, totally different from the hell in Dallas. I grabbed an umbrella and set out for a walk.

I wandered along the seawall along the lake into Old Toronto. With my mask, I could barely smell the lake. They kept saying they were going to ban dumping pollutants into Lake Ontario, but they had been saying that for two hundred years. As long as someone made money off it, the corps did what they wanted.

Past the entertainment district, I turned inland and made my way around the sewage treatment plant toward the old tenement building where Amanda Rollins had her orphanage. The corporate types never saw that part of town, nor did the corporations provide any services to the people who lived there. Neither the subway nor the buses ran there, and they had to pay scamming resellers for electricity and water at far higher rates than people paid in the corporate parts of town.

I passed a small store with a beggar out front. Across the street, none of the windows in the house had glass. I wouldn't see any more beggars on my route. No one bothered to beg from people who didn't have anything.

Picking my way through rubble in the street where an old burned building had fallen down, I heard whistles—signals between gang members that an outsider had entered their territory. It was rare that someone who could afford shoes went into that part of town. Most of the people who lived there couldn't even afford filter masks and had to breathe the raw air. Even with my skills, the danger was very real. My mask alone made me worth mugging. The corporations employed the police, but they paid them to keep the inhabitants in the slums, not to control their behavior.

"I'm a friend of Miz Rollins," I shouted and continued walking as though I didn't have a care in the world.

A couple of blocks farther on, a dirty-faced girl of about fifteen stepped out of an alley ahead of me, her skinny legs poking out from what used to be a blue floral-print shift. Her ragged hair might have been blonde if it had been clean.

"Miz Libby?" she called. She looked ready to bolt.

I smiled. "Hello, Glenda. How have you been?"

A big smile split her face. "I been pretty good." She skipped toward me.

Crouching down, I opened my arms and gathered her into a hug.

"You been gone," she said.

"Yes, I know. I'm a bum." I pulled a package of beef jerky out of my pocket and handed it to her.

"You're not a bum. You're the best." She tore open the package, stuffed a wad of the dried meat in her mouth, and fell in beside me.

"The boys been bothering you?" I asked.

"Not too bad. Jorey keeps em off me."

49

I controlled a flare of temper. "That's nice of Jorey," I managed to say. I didn't know Jorey, but I doubted he was an altruist.

"I'm nice to him, and he's nice to me. He never hurts me and he say he'll keep me warm this winter. You goin to see Miz Rollins?"

Glenda got tired of her alcoholic mother selling her for booze and drug money, and ran away when she was twelve. It wasn't much better on the street. I met her when I stumbled over two older teens taking turns with her in an alley. Those two, and three more over time, served as a warning to others that tumbling the little blonde girl could carry a death sentence. Most of the street people stayed away from her after that. I couldn't save all the thousands of girls living on the streets, but I figured that shouldn't stop me from killing all the rapists I could get my hands on.

Like most of the people in that part of town, Glenda couldn't read or write. She had been to a doctor once in her life, when I took her to get all her immunizations and an implant. In spite of all the constantly mutating diseases, Glenda amazingly hadn't caught any. During my sex-ed class in middle school, the teacher told us scientists identified a new sexually transmitted disease every week that were mostly caused by mutations of known pathogens. In spite of growing up in a brothel, those classes made me so paranoid I was still a virgin when I got to university.

Nellie kept telling me I should take Glenda to my mom. With regular nutrition and hygiene, she would be pretty. It would be a better life, but the thought of her in a brothel turned my stomach. Maybe Nellie was right, though. It would be better than leaving her to the tender mercies of whoever the hell Jorey was. She'd at least have a chance at a decent life.

We arrived at the orphanage, and the place erupted, kids screaming and running around.

"Miz Libby!"

"It's Miz Libby!"

"Miz Rollins, it's Miz Libby!"

Most of the kids were able at least to dress and feed themselves. They were all either crippled or disfigured, some so severely they might face harm in the richer parts of town just because of the way they looked.

One boy who couldn't take care of himself was Walter. *Hello, Miz Libby,* Walter's voice sounded in my head. *I hope you're doing well.*

Walter was blind and confined to a wheelchair, but he was the most powerful telepath I had ever met. Of course, I hadn't met too many.

Amanda Rollins came to the door and waved, a broad smile on her face. Amanda was a tall, thin, light-skinned black woman. I figured she was in her forties but she appeared older. She was the only person in my life that I knew was going to heaven.

We embraced and went inside to the kitchen. She shooed everyone out and closed the door.

"Libby, it's good to see you." She shook her head. "That money you sent with Nellie, I don't know how I can ever thank you. Dear Lord, that's more money than I ran this place on all of last year. If it wasn't for you, I think everything would just fall apart. You're an angel, girl. An angel from heaven."

"I've been accused of a lot of things," I said, "but that's a first. I'm no angel, and I'm definitely no saint. That's you."

Amanda was Nellie's aunt, and that's how I met her. I emptied my bag of the stuff I brought. Beef jerky, dried fruit, children's vitamins, basic medicines, such as aspirin, alcohol, hydrogen peroxide, sterile gauze and surgical tape.

"Oh, Lord," Amanda said. "It don't matter what you show up with, it's always something I need that I don't have."

The building didn't have electricity, therefore no refrigeration. How she managed always amazed me.

I pulled out the credit card Dad had given me for Carpenter's jewelry and her eyes popped wide.

"I want you to move someplace with electricity," I said. "I want you out of this neighborhood. And I want you to have a doctor come regularly, at least once a month."

"Oh, Libby. I can't afford all that."

"You can now." I handed her my dad's business card. "Call this man and tell him I sent you. Tell him how big a place you need, a place with electricity and heat in the winter. Tell him you can pay a thousand a month, but no more."

"A thousand a month? There ain't no way I can afford that. I never seen a thousand a month my whole life."

"Tell him I'm paying the rent."

Her mouth fell open.

"I'll pay the utilities, too. Now, this," I held out the card again, "is for furniture, food, medicines, doctors, all the other things you'll need. Let me know when you're ready to move, and I'll bring some friends and a truck to help." I couldn't think of a better place to spend Kahlil Carpenter's money, although it was probably his insurance company's money.

She shook her head so hard I thought she might sprain something. "No, no, no. Libby, you don't know

52

how much all that will cost. How am I going to keep things going after you spend all your money? Your heart's in the right place, child, but you got no sense."

I slid the card into her shirt pocket. "I set up an account with a hundred thousand, Amanda. When it runs dry, I'll put some more in it. And tell Jason, when he finds the building, to send the rent and utility bills to me." I figured the money would last years. I was sure Amanda wouldn't know how to spend a hundred thousand credits.

I was doing pretty good up until then, but when the tears started running down her face, I almost lost it.

"Hey, I gotta go. One thing, though. You know this Jorey that Glenda's hanging with?"

"Sure, I know him."

"Where would I find him?"

"You don't want to. Damned gangbanger."

"He's in a gang?"

"He runs a gang. The Eastside Boys. Girls, drugs, extortion."

"How old is he?"

"I dunno. Nineteen, twenty maybe. Stay away from him. He's bad news."

"Thanks." I gave her a hug and fled. I don't do well with tears and thank yous.

On my way out, I grabbed Glenda. "You want to go live someplace that's warm all the time? Three meals a day? Shoes?"

She stared at me as though I'd grown another head.

"Well?"

"You're gonna 'dopt me?"

Damn. Careful Libby. "No, I'm going to take you someplace that will give you a job and teach you to read and write. Someone who owes me a favor."

"Is he nice?"

My heart about broke right then and there. Glenda categorized men as nice or not nice, depending on whether they enjoyed hurting her when they raped her.

"No, honey, it's a woman, and she won't ever ask you to take off your clothes and be nice to men."

"Sure," she said with a perky smile. "Will I still see you sometimes?"

"You'll see me more often."

She reached out and took my hand. "We shouldn't tell Jorey I'm leaving. I think he'll be mad."

⊕⊕⊕

As we passed into the nicer parts of the city, I noticed a number of people giving us some strange looks. Glenda was filthy and she stank. When we got to Mom's place, I took Glenda around back and knocked on the kitchen door. The dishwasher answered.

"What do you want?"

"I need to see Lilith."

"Go to the front. You can't come in here."

"Call Dominik, please." The chef knew what I looked like in my regular form as well as the redheaded form. A lot of Mom's employees thought she had two daughters, the nice redhead named Lizzie, and me.

The dishwasher sneered at me, but turned and

yelled for Dominik, who came over.

"I need to see Mom," I said. I wasn't sure he heard me because he was staring so hard at Glenda. I didn't care. Taking her hand, I walked up the steps and into the kitchen. Dominik backed up out of my way.

"Thank you," I told him with a smile. I dragged Glenda through the kitchen as quickly as I could. I didn't think her smell would affect any of the food, but better not to take the chance. As for her, she simply gaped at everything. I think she was as stunned as Dominik.

The office door was open, so I presented myself with Glenda behind me.

"Hi, Mom. I need a favor."

"All right," she said, pushing her chair back from the desk. "Do I get to hear what it is before I agree to it?"

"Not really. Just say yes and then I'll explain."

She threw her head back and laughed. "Who the hell taught you the art of negotiation?"

"You did. See how well I paid attention?"

I stepped into the office, pulling Glenda with me. Mom stared at her even more incredulously than Dominik had.

"No." She seemed to be trying to say something else, but in the end she just repeated, "No."

"She needs a job," I said. "Dishwasher, scrub the floors, clean the rooms, take out the trash, anything. She'll work for room and board, and she needs to learn to read and write. That's all I'm asking."

"No. Good God, Libby. What in the hell were you thinking?"

I bit my lip, took a deep breath and looked down at Glenda's crestfallen expression. I realized how

55

stupid I'd been in building up the girl's hopes. For the first time in years, I wanted to cry.

"Fine. I'll just take her back and dump her on the street. The gangs and other predators will be glad to have her back. No big deal. We'll just wash our hands of her. Would you like to contribute to the burial fund, or isn't that important either? Just let her rot after they rape her to death?"

I didn't know who was more shocked, Glenda or my mom. They stared at me with identical expressions of horror. Mom closed her eyes, and I could see her face twitching and moving. When she opened her eyes, I could see they were filmy with tears.

"Damn you," Mom said. "Other people's kids bring home kittens and puppies. Who is she? Where the hell did you find her?"

I gave her a brief history of how I met Glenda and gotten to know her over the past couple of years. "Mom, Nellie suggested bringing her here over a year ago. I'm not asking you to train her to be one of your girls. Just give her a chance. She needs a stable environment, and Lord knows, she can't stay with me. She's a good girl, honest."

"I don't steal," Glenda said in a tiny voice. "Miz Rollins says Jesus say stealing is wrong."

A single tear escaped my mother's eye. She wiped it away and said, "I'll take her on a trial basis. But you, missy, will be involved. You're not just dumping her on me and then wander off on your merry way. You want her to read and write? You're going to help teach her."

"Thanks, Mom. Glenda, this is Lettie, but when other people are around, you should call her Miss Lilith. Okay?"

"Yes, ma'am. Thank you, Miz Lettie. I'll be good. I

don't take up much space and I don't eat much."

"I can see that," Mom said, "but I think we can fix it. Come on. Let's go find you a place to stay and a bath."

She led us to a room over the kitchen, near the back stairs. It had a bed, a dresser and a bathroom.

"Libby, take that dress out and burn it," Mom said. "I don't even want to touch it. Then while she takes a bath, you can go buy her some clothes."

"Take off your dress, Glenda," I prompted. The girl pulled the shift over her head. She was completely nude under it, and Mom and I both stared. I could not only count her ribs, but every bone in her body. I knew she was thin, but not on the verge of starvation.

Mom triggered the intercom. "Dominik, I'm in room twenty-three. Send me up a milk shake made with fruit."

"Small or large?" Dominik's voice replied.

"Small, but I may want another one in a couple of hours."

"Should I expect one more person for meals?" he asked.

"Yes. Thank you." Mom turned to me. "What are you waiting for? Get rid of that rag." She went into the bathroom and started running water in the tub. "Glenda, come here."

Glenda looked at me and I nodded. "Do whatever she tells you. She's my mother, Glenda, and my best friend. You don't have to be afraid."

I picked up the shift with my thumb and one finger. Holding it at arm's length, I took it down the back stairs and pitched it in the dumpster in the alley. A store that sold clothing was four blocks away, and I bought two weeks' worth of underwear, a couple of training bras, a few dresses, tops and pants, and a pair of sandals. I could estimate the clothing, but not the shoe size, so I figured I'd take her for shoes later. I also picked up a couple of filter masks. I shuddered to think of how much damage her lungs had suffered, even at her age.

When I got back, Glenda was sitting in the tub sucking on a straw in a milkshake, and Mom was torturing her with a hairbrush.

"Hey, don't do that," I said. "Just cut it all off. It'll grow back." The bath water was cleaner than I expected.

"That's the second bath," Mom said. "She turned the water black the first time around." She stood up straight and stared down at the girl, then at the hairbrush. "You're probably right. I'm half afraid of what I might find in that mop."

"I would suspect lice," I said. "Hopefully nothing worse."

"I'll be right back. When she finishes that shake, explain the proper use of soap again. I'm not sure she understood the first lesson." Mom dumped the brush in the bath and left the room.

Two hours later, we had a pretty young lady with a shining face and half-inch-long blonde hair. Dominik had brought a second milk shake and she was industriously sucking away at it. With her free hand, she kept stroking her new maroon cotton dress as though it was precious.

"My God, Libby," Mom sighed. "She actually looks like a human being."

⊕⊕⊕

58

CHAPTER 6

I dumped my clothes in the washer on the way to the shower. From the moment I hugged Glenda, I'd known that smell would cling to me. By the time I emerged, smelling of shampoo and conditioner, I realized I hadn't eaten all day and I was starving.

I called Nellie. She answered on the second ring and told me Richard was doing a family night. We agreed to meet at our favorite restaurant.

An Poteen Stil, an Irish pub, served the best burgers and fish and chips in Toronto, along with the best beer and whisky. It was independently owned, not a corporate chain, and the grandson of the man who first opened the place tended the bar. I loved that it had a large dance floor and traditional Irish music seven nights a week.

We were sharing a bread pudding dessert when a man stopped at our table. I looked up and saw it was Ron, the guy I met the night Adnan tried to kidnap me. He was wearing a t-shirt, and both arms were sleeved in tattoos.

"Hello," I said, trying to smile, talk, and swallow at the same time. I'm always classy like that.

"Hi, how are you?" He looked from me to Nellie and back. "So this is where the blues diva comes on her night off."

Nellie winked at him. "You've discovered my secret."

"You with someone?" I asked.

"No, just stopped in for dinner and a pint."

I indicated an empty chair. "You can join us if you like."

Nellie leaned over and whispered in my ear.

"There you go again, playing hard to get." Luckily, I wasn't drinking when she said it.

He sat down and ordered when the waitress came over.

"Do you know how to dance to this music?" I asked him.

"I sure do," he said with a chuckle. "Do you Irish dance?"

"I've had a few lessons. Are you a good teacher?"

We spun out onto the dance floor. I had liked dancing to R and B with him. He was even better at céilí and set dancing.

"You were sandbagging me," he said after the first song.

I laughed. "My grandmother was Irish. My mother danced competitively when she was young."

"Can you step dance?" he asked.

"Yes, but I'm not that good. I don't get to practice much."

After another song, the waitress brought his food, and we went back to the table. Nellie gave me a knowing smirk.

We stuck around for a couple of hours and Ron did give Nellie a couple of dance lessons, but mainly he and I danced. I was nowhere near tired, but eventually he said that he needed to go to work the next day.

"Where do you work?" Nellie asked.

"Um..." he suddenly seemed wary, as if ashamed, or maybe afraid we would laugh or think he was uncool.

"It's okay," I said. "It's one of those if-I-tell-you,-I'll-have-to-kill-you jobs. Right?"

"Not exactly, but some people get grossed out."

"Ewww," Nellie said. "You're the guy who cleans the sewers?"

He laughed. "Not that bad. I work at a funeral home."

Nellie barked out a laugh and opened her mouth to say something, but I kicked her under the table.

"Don't let her visit you at work," I said. "She's a closet necrophiliac."

"I am not!"

As we watched him walk away, and we definitely watched, Nellie said, "You like him, huh?"

"I like dancing with him. I don't know anything about him, though."

"What's there to know? If he can translate those moves from vertical to horizontal, you've got a winner."

⊕⊕⊕

A week after I finished the Sholokhov assignment, my doorbell rang. Only a half-dozen people knew where I lived, and my parents never came over. They summoned me if they desired the pleasure of my company.

I slipped on a hoodie over the t-shirt and shorts I wore and put my pistol in the pocket, then opened the door. The man in an expensive suit was a stranger.

"May I help you?" I asked.

"Miss Nelson?"

"Mister?"

His smile tightened a little and I saw a brief flash in his eyes, but he responded pleasantly. "I'm sorry.

My name is Gareth Blaine." He pulled out a corporate ID and held it up. "I represent the Chamber of Commerce." He had a British accent.

Holy smokes. What kind of trouble was I in now? After the wars, the corporations decided that governments could no longer be trusted with anything important. Of course, most governments were corporately controlled already, but nukes falling out of the sky were bad for business. The corporations stopped pretending and relegated governments to what they saw as their proper role. The rule of law became a joke. Instead of laws, contracts between corporations ruled society, and the arbiters of those contracts were the Chamber of Commerce, the Court of International Trade, and the Board of International Settlements.

"Yes, I'm Elizabeth Nelson."

"May I come in? I'd like to discuss a business proposition."

I showed him in, offered him something to drink, then sat on the edge of a chair wondering what the hell his visit was about.

"I understand that you recently provided services to Mr. and Mrs. Simon Wellington."

"Mr. Blaine, my services are in the area of personal and property security. I'm sure you understand that confidentiality and discretion are required. I am not at liberty to discuss either my clients or any services I might have provided."

I was sweating bullets. I might be able to run and hide from an individual corporation, but if the Chamber was after me, getting on a plane would be almost impossible. My only option would be the backwoods, and I am so not a country girl.

"I completely understand," Blaine said. "It was

Mr. Wellington who recommended you."

The tension flowed out of me. I wondered if Blaine could sense my relief.

He continued. "Mr. Wellington said that you were familiar with the luvdaze problem."

"A little. I've run into it during an investigation, and I've read about it."

He nodded. "I'm going to be blunt. We think the drug is being manufactured here, in Toronto. It's being marketed to a very different demographic than we're used to seeing, and I don't have any agents who could easily infiltrate the circles where it's being used and sold. We tried recruiting a couple of university students to go undercover, and they ended up dead."

I may not be the brightest light, but it was pretty evident where the conversation was headed.

"And what makes you think I would fare any better?"

"You're Jason Bouchard's daughter."

Well, that was pretty blunt.

"Miss Nelson, I've known your father for twenty-five years. After his accident, after he retired, I have contracted services through him on behalf of my employers. You're young and fit the demographic. You're smart, and the fact that you're running a successful security business is evidence that your father trained you."

"Have you spoken to him about this?"

"No. I'm following up on Simon Wellington's suggestion that we enlist your help." He gave a slight shrug. "I don't mind you discussing it with Jason, as long as our confidentiality is kept."

Unable to sit still any longer, I jumped up and paced across the room. "Exactly what do you want me to do?"

"Try and find out who is producing and distributing this junk. I'll make any resources you need available to you."

I thought about it. It wasn't that I'd never earned any legitimate money, but usually my work was on the decidedly shady side. Being one of the good guys wasn't a familiar role. On the other hand, being in good with the Chamber couldn't hurt me. I might even be able to pull a string or two if I ever got caught with my hand in the cookie jar.

On the third hand, the assignment itself had tons of downside. I considered dying a significant downside. The possibility of a painful death was even more disturbing. I'm not a pain girl. A little light spanking was the extent of my masochism, and you'd better make sure I had a couple of drinks first.

"You said resources. If I need any technology, do I get to keep it after the assignment?"

I caught him by surprise, as evidenced by his bark of laughter. "It depends," he said with a chuckle. "I'm not buying you a helicopter or a laser cannon."

With a grin, I said, "Shucks. I've always wanted my own laser cannon." I walked back to my chair and sat down. "Electronics were more what I had in mind. Surveillance equipment, jammers, see-through technology. The kind of sophisticated stuff that's not readily available on the open market. I'd also want my own cavalry."

His brow furrowed. "Cavalry?"

"You know, tough guys ready to ride to my rescue. I'm pretty slippery, but I have a congenital aversion to pain and death. If I get into something I can't get out of, I want to know someone has my back."

"You want us to monitor you," he said slowly.

"Yes. You're going to anyway. I just want an open arrangement. Communication."

He leaned back in his chair and looked me over. "I'm a bit surprised. You normally work alone."

"I normally don't do this kind of work. I don't want you hanging over my shoulder, or insisting on daily reports, but I would appreciate knowing I'm not walking into a drug den alone with no options." I leaned forward with my elbows on my knees. "Mr. Blaine, I may be young, but I've never taken drugs. Any illegal drugs. I've never been in the drug culture. You're going to have to insert me as a novice. Miss Goody Two-Shoes gets in over her head type of thing."

"We can do that. I can get you a university ID."

I nodded. "That would be good. University of Calgary under a different identity. I'll get you pictures. Now, as to pay. My normal services don't include risking my neck. Triple my normal rates plus expenses."

He shocked me. I expected him to haggle. I'd have been happy with anything over my normal rates. Nellie and Amanda would have a coronary if they knew what I was asking for this job.

"I'll have the contract drawn up," Blaine said. "Is tomorrow at this time convenient? Can you have the pictures by then?"

After he left, I paced around the house. What in the hell was I doing? I'd scrupulously avoided drugs my whole life. I knew nothing about the drug culture. Would I have to take them? Crap. I might be willing to try something mild, like weed, but not luvdaze or heroin.

Maybe it would be better to go at it another way.

Provide some money and present myself as a seller. That might work. Poor little rich girl chafing under the limits of daddy's allowance. Maybe a little awkward, wanting to fit in. Yeah, a nerd. A lot easier for me to pull off than a femme fatale. That could help to explain my fear of the drug. Nerd loses virginity under luvdaze, only wants to do it with boyfriend.

I went to my bedroom and stood in front of a mirror. First, change the hair to black. Leave the height alone, maybe a little more boobage and butt. That worked. Then the face. Not homely, but a bit more plain. Widen the nose, thicken the lips, flatten the cheekbones, round out the face and chin. Give a bit of a slant to the eyes and take off a few years so I'd look university age. I played with it a bit and found something that fit the nerd-girl stereotype. Some stupid t-shirts could round out the image. Being over six feet tall when I was fourteen gave me plenty of practice feeling awkward, especially around boys.

When I had what I wanted, I took the ID pictures. I could have created my own identification. Dad taught me forgery when I was barely a teen, but I didn't see any reason to let Blaine know that.

Blaine. He said he'd contracted services from Dad. I doubted those services had to do with stealing jewelry. Maybe industrial espionage, but that was more a corporate concern, not the Chamber's. That meant he'd probably contracted for assassinations.

I got dressed and headed over to my father's house.

⊕⊕⊕

Dad listened to my story, then said, "Yes, I know Gareth Blaine, and I trust him about as far as I can throw him."

"So you think I made a mistake agreeing to help him?"

"Damned lousy business." He took a deep breath. "No, I don't think you had much of a choice. I mean, you could have turned him down, but he'd have been mad. He's used to getting his way. But be damned careful, Libby. Remember, he's grasping at straws. No one else has any ideas of what to do about this drug mess, so if you can't figure it out either, that's not a strike against you."

"Does he know I do wet work?" I asked. Wet work was the euphemism used for assassinations.

"I think he suspects, or he wouldn't have approached you. When he told you his previous operatives died, and you didn't flinch, you basically confirmed it. Most rational people stay far away from death."

"You're saying I'm not rational."

He shook his head. "No, you're not. It's my fault, but I'm not apologizing. Your parents are criminals, and we raised you to be a criminal because we don't feel guilty about what we've done. You're my legacy. Out of all my kills, only a couple caused me any heartache, and they were collateral damage. To tell you the truth, Libby, if someone shot the chiefs of every corporation in the world, I wouldn't shed a tear. Do you want to know why?"

"Yeah. I mean, it's better than the old system, isn't it? Crazy people with armies dropping bombs on cities?"

"I'm not saying the old way was better, but this oligarchical system is very close to a type of slavery. People like us, the indies, are the only reason the corps haven't enslaved everyone. That and laziness.

But my major gripe with them is this—look at the wealth Simon Wellington has, and then look at your friend Amanda Rollins. Which one do you think deserves to live? But the corps are killing her. Slowly to be sure, but it's a shitty system."

"Did Amanda call you?"

"Yes. Why are you doing this?"

I started to get defensive. "It's my money. I earned it and I can spend it any way I like."

"I'm not disputing that. I'm just asking why."

I bit my lip and tried to formulate my thoughts in a way he'd understand. "Dad, those kids didn't ask to be born, and they sure didn't ask to be born the way they are. They've had the shittiest end of the stick poked in their eyes, but you'd never know it when you meet them. They're sweet and kind to each other. They smile, and none of them has any reason to smile. Like you said, some people got nothing, and some have everything. I have more money than I need. Why not help someone else?"

"You're not doing it because you feel guilty about the people you've killed? You're not trying to assuage your guilt, are you?"

"Phaw! Oh, hell no. Dad, when I bring food to those kids and they love me for it, it makes me feel good. It makes me feel happy. I mean, I know you and Mom love me, but I like having someone else love me, too. It makes me feel that I'm earning the oxygen I'm using."

He cracked a smile. "And that's the best reason in the world for doing something. Okay, I found her a building, an old school. I had it inspected, and it's structurally sound. Electricity and running water just have to be turned on. Has a kitchen and cafeteria, but someone will need to clean up and refinish the kitchen equipment. Some of it might have to be replaced. The catch is, it's not for rent, but you can buy it for cheap."

I opened my mouth and then stopped. I hadn't considered buying something. I thought it would be a lot more expensive. "Can I get a mortgage?"

"Probably. You don't have the credit, but I'd co-sign it. Do it on fifteen years and the monthly payments would probably be around five hundred."

I leaped out of my chair and gave him a big hug. "You are the best."

"I take it that's a yes?"

⊕⊕⊕

Blaine came by the next day. I gave him the pictures of me and ran the contract through a software program to check it. We haggled over a couple of the provisions, but in the end he made the changes I asked for, we initialed them, and then we signed it. I wasn't a corporate employee, but it was as close as I'd ever been.

"These are the pictures for the IDs?" he asked, examining them closely. "You can actually look like this?"

"Yeah. I put on the disguise before I took them."

"You're pretty damn good. You could make a living doing makeup for vids."

Only for a one-woman show.

"I've heard lots of stories about drug gangs," I said. "I don't want anyone deciding to take revenge on me later."

"I can understand that. I should have the documentation for you by tomorrow. When can you

69

start?"

"As soon as I have the IDs, I'll rent a cheap flat down by the university and bill it on my invoice."

I told him about my idea of going after the drugs as a dealer rather than a user. "I doubt the people selling this stuff are using it," I said. "From what I can tell, it's pretty debilitating."

"You're right about that. It's the same with most hard drugs. The dealers at the lowest levels tend to be users trying to support their habits, but above them, it's all business."

"Kind of what I thought."

CHAPTER 7

I went down to The Pinnacle that evening to hear Nellie sing and tell her about the school for Miz Rollins. I also told her I had a gig and wouldn't be around much.

I'd been there for about an hour when Ron came in, ordered one of those ugly orange things at the bar, and came over to my table.

"Hi," I said. "Have a seat." He did. "I have no idea how you can drink that stuff."

"I guess it's an acquired taste. An old girlfriend of mine used to drink them."

"Did they kill her? Is that why she's ex?"

He laughed. "No, she said she couldn't handle my job. Said that she thought about death all the time when she was with me."

"I think about death a lot, too. I think about all the assholes I'd like to kill."

He laughed again. "I hope I'm not one of them."

"No, I think you're okay. I haven't seen you being an asshole. Wanna dance?" Nellie often commented on my subtle approach with men. I just had a hard time putting myself out there the way she did. I guessed I was destined to be a wallflower.

Nellie was in a mood that night, singing a lot of slow songs. We danced a fast one, then when the next one was slow, I flowed into his arms. I like to think I flowed. It sounds better than 'awkwardly stumbled into him.'

After a minute or so of us being pressed together, he said, "God, you feel good."

"Yeah, I do. How did you know?"

He seemed to think I was funny, and I liked his

71

laugh.

"Keep playing your cards right, my boy, and all you see before you could be yours someday," I said with mock seriousness.

"I have to work tomorrow," he said, "but maybe we could go on a date sometime."

"You mean, like a get-dressed-up, go-out-to-dinner, boy-and-girl-alone kind of thing?"

"Something like that."

"Wow, you really have this romance thing down. I'm more used to hearing, 'You girl, me boy. Let's fuck.'"

"Oh? And does that work?"

"About as well as you'd expect."

The song came to an end, and he twirled me around, pulled me close, and kissed me on the lips. It didn't shock me, but it left me speechless. He took my hand and led me back to our table. As I sat down, I glanced at the stage. Nellie gave me a big smile and a thumbs-up.

I thought about the kiss, decided it wasn't too shabby, took a swallow of my beer, and asked, "So what are your days off?"

"Tuesday and Wednesday."

"Slow days for dying?"

"Slow days for funerals. People prefer weekends so they don't have to take off work."

"Makes sense. Well?"

"Well, what?"

"Are you going to ask me on a date?"

I started laughing uncontrollably as he got up from his chair, knelt down in front of me, took my hand and said, "Miss Libby, would you do me the honor of going to dinner with me this coming Tuesday evening?"

"Get up. People are looking."

"Not until you agree to make this the happiest Tuesday of my life."

"Oh, God. Don't push it, bud. Yes, I'll go to dinner with you on Tuesday. Now get up."

I waved Nellie over when she took a break. "Are you going to see Miz Rollins soon?"

"Probably tomorrow. Tom and I were going to drop by the orphanage." Tom was Nellie's older brother and about the size of a small mountain. He was one of the bouncers at Pinnacle.

"Tell her that we found a building. I'll stop by sometime next week and take her to see it."

"I can't believe you're doing that."

"I'm trying to buy my way into heaven," I said. "I think I can manage that easier than being good."

She punched me in the shoulder. "What kind of building?"

"Dad says it's an old school."

She got excited all of a sudden. "Where is it?"

I told her and she said, "I know it. It's six blocks from my mother's house. I went to school there. They closed it about five years ago. It's in pretty good shape."

Nellie had told me she went to school through eighth grade. The neighborhood got older, and fewer children meant fewer parents to pay. Eventually the school closed.

After she went back on stage, I asked Ron, "Did you go to school?"

"Oh, yeah. My family's been in the funeral

73

business for generations. I didn't go to university, but I went to a good school. Almost as good as a corporate school. What about you?"

"Yeah, that's about like me," I lied. The only thing my grandmother ever did for me was put me in a top prep school and the University of Toronto. I guess as angry as they were at Mom when they cut her off, they couldn't stand the thought of seeing me as a servant. That probably would be awkward, going to your snotty friends' house and seeing your granddaughter scrubbing their floor.

"So, where do you want me to meet you Tuesday?" I asked.

Ron's eyes widened in surprise. "I figured I'd pick you up."

I shook my head. "No addresses on a first date. You have a car?"

"Motorcycle. Why? Afraid of stalkers?"

"You ride a motorcycle? So do I. Maybe we can take a ride together sometime." I liked him more all the time. "Place?" I prompted.

"Aldo's? You like Italian?"

"I like food. Aldo's is nice. It's quiet, good for conversation."

"Seven o'clock," he said as he stood.

I reached up, grabbed his shirt and pulled his head down. The kiss he'd given me on the dance floor was pleasant, but quick. By the time I let him up for air, his flushed face displayed the same disorientation as mine probably did.

"Tuesday, seven o'clock," I said. "I'll even wear a dress and brush my hair."

⊕⊕⊕

The doorbell sounded at the crack of dawn. I tried to ignore it, hoping the idiot would go away. No luck, the bell kept ringing. Stumbling out of bed, I grabbed my pistol. Anyone calling at that time of the morning had already proven themselves an enemy.

It was Blaine.

"Do you know what time it is?"

"Yes," he said, "it's nine thirty." The only reason I didn't shoot him was because he held out a carryout cup of coffee. I cautiously took it and sniffed it. Caramel mocha. He was still a bastard, but I let him live.

Inhaling the fumes and taking small sips as I sat on the couch, I gave him the evil eye. "What the hell is so important that it can't wait until noon?" I asked.

He held out a handful of documents in hard copy and several chips—student ID, corporate ID, passport, transcripts, birth certificate. Jasmine Keller had everything except a boyfriend. The pictures I'd given Blaine were on every document that needed them.

"You have this identity flagged in your systems," I said.

"Of course. She's entered and validated across the board."

"Take off the flags. Make her anonymous."

He blinked at me. Then he blinked again.

"This," I held up all the documents, "is mine. She's not yours. She's available to me after this contract, without any flags. Fix it. I'll know if you don't."

"Well...I mean...we've contracted you..." he stuttered.

"Your password on your personal account is

75

capital x, yz5347602," I said. "Your validation question answer is Helen, a name I'm sure your ex-wife would be interested in. I'll know if you leave any flags on this identity."

Probably not the smartest or most diplomatic way to start a relationship with a client, but I was groggy. I hated him for waking me up, and I suddenly felt a need to establish who was in charge. He might be paying me, but I wasn't his lackey.

He stared at me for some time, his face set in stone and his eyes angry. "I'll take care of it," he finally said.

"Good. I assume you have a dossier on this case for me to read.

He handed me a chip.

"Thanks. Are my contact numbers and addresses on this?"

He nodded.

"Send my guardian angel over at one o'clock so we can work out the details."

"I'm sorry. Details?" Blaine must have been slow that morning.

"Code words, when and where we'll communicate, when he'll charge in to save the day and when he won't. You know, that sort of minor details. Mr. Blaine, I hope you've assigned the A team to cover me. If this guy is an idiot..." I let my sentence die.

"You're pretty damned cocky," he said. That was the second time I'd provoked him to anger. I made a note that he wasn't as sure of himself as he tried to project. If I was in his position, I'd be a lot more confident.

"We can walk away from this deal right now," I said. "You're the one who solicited me. Either we deal as equal partners, or we don't deal at all."

He silently regarded me, then sighed. "You're right," he said. "I'll send Wilbur over at one."

Wilbur?

⊕⊕⊕

Wilbur Wilberforce had parents with a bizarre sense of humor. On the other hand, I certainly wasn't going to make fun of his name. Six feet five inches with shoulders he had to turn to get through the door, he had a shaved head, dark eyes, golden-brown skin, and the kind of chiseled face the entertainment industry favored for action heroes. His arms rippled with muscle, and his six pack had a six pack. I guessed he was about ten years older than I was.

With my usual aplomb, I opened the door and stared at him with my mouth agape. Before I started to drool, he said in a baritone voice that caused various parts of my anatomy to heat up, "Miss Nelson? I'm Wilbur Wilberforce. Mr. Blaine sent me."

"Of course," I stammered. "Won't you come in?" As he passed through the door, I wondered whether I was quick enough to hit the floor first if I tripped him.

"Can I get you something to drink?"

"Water, if you please. Thank you."

I tried to think of something else to ask him just so I could hear his voice. Where had this man been all my life? The answer was pretty obvious. Spending his time being chased by super models and vid stars. Get hold of yourself, Libby. Even in my natural form, I couldn't compete for a guy like him, let alone wearing Jasmine's form, which I'd put on for our meeting. I doubted an awkward nerd would ring his bell.

77

I brought him a glass of water.

"Mr. Blaine said you wanted to get together to coordinate your protection," Wilbur said.

"Uh, yeah." I stopped, seized hold of my libido, strangled it, and stuffed it in a hole deep in my mind where it continued to pant and drool. Taking a breath, I said, "I think we should each understand the other's understanding of our relationship. Don't you agree?" Why did I use the word relationship? Partnership? What the hell word should I use that didn't set off unwelcome visions in my mind?

Luckily, Wilbur was professional. He asked what my plan was. We discussed several aspects of it, and he made a couple of good suggestions. Neither of us thought this investigation would be quick or easy.

"You do know that drug investigations sometimes take months, if not years?" he asked.

Did that mean we should move in together? My libido asked, but I stomped on it again.

We worked out code words for various scenarios and actions, and he gave me an earpiece to keep in contact with him. He told me it contained a tracker, and showed me how to shut the audio off.

"You're starting tonight?" he asked.

"Yes, but just preliminary scouting runs. I know one club where the stuff is being peddled, but I want to find out how widespread it is. A friend of mine runs The Pinnacle, and although I've never noticed much of a drug scene there, their clientele fits the older end of the demographic."

He nodded. "I assume you won't be wearing your disguise for that," he said. "Do you want me following you when you're Elizabeth Nelson, or only as Jasmine Keller?"

Ooo, good question.

"Suppose I tell you when I don't need you? I have a date tomorrow night. I don't think that would be comfortable for either of us." Let alone Ron.

Wilbur nodded. "That makes sense."

"Tonight, I'll go to The Pinnacle as myself. Did Blaine give you a picture?" Wilbur nodded again. "I'll be asking a lot of questions, and I'd appreciate your noticing if anyone seems to pay too much attention to me."

"All right. I'll see you there tonight. Turn your comm link on so we can test it."

"Thanks for stopping by, Wilbur."

For the first time, he smiled, and as I melted into a puddle on the floor, he said, "Just call me Wil."

⊕⊕⊕

Never one to let logic and reality interfere with my dreams, I dressed and did my hair and makeup as though Wil would actually be interested in me and set out for The Pinnacle. An inconsiderate witch in the back of my mind nagged that if he fell for any woman at the club, it would be Nellie. It had happened before. But if he did, then he'd still come around for me to stare at and drool over.

I didn't see him when I walked into the club, but he came through the door just when I reached the bar and turned around. If he was following me, he was good. I'd been more vigilant than usual, knowing I might have a tail. Dressed to go clubbing, he was even more incredible than he'd been that afternoon.

"Oh, wow," I heard Paul's voice behind me. I turned and saw he was staring past me toward the door.

"You could give me a complex," I said.

"Oh, hi, Libby. God, did you see that guy over there?"

"Yes, Paul, I saw him. Get in line. By the time he gets his first drink, half the club will be drooling on him."

"You know him?" He sounded hopeful.

"No, I don't, and I doubt I'll ever get the chance to. Give me a beer."

Paul came back with my drink and I asked him, "Do you think there's much drug dealing in here?"

He snorted and stared at me with a puzzled grin on his face. "Duh. Haven't you been paying attention?"

"I guess not. You know I don't do that sort of thing."

He put his elbows on the bar and leaned toward me. "We make sure it stays low key because we want to keep our image up. People go to the bathrooms or outside to do it. But yeah, the younger corporate generation spends half its time spending money, and the other half blowing their brains out with drugs and screwing. Why? Are you feeling left out?"

Paul and I met in grammar school and been fast friends ever since. He knew more about me than almost anyone. He was my best friend when I discovered my chameleon abilities. His older brothers had gone the heavy corporate route like their dad, but Paul was more laid back. Manager of a corporate bar was more his style than running the finances on the entire chain. I'd skipped The Pinnacle in Dallas in favor of the mutie bars. It wouldn't be the same without Paul and Nellie.

80

"What do you know about luvdaze?"

He straightened. "Whoa. Libby, if you want to take a walk on the wild side, you should start with something a little safer. You don't want to get involved with that stuff. I can score you some weed or coke."

"Thanks. If I ever want to scramble my neurons, I'll let you know. I'm just curious. I had a client whose son is doing luvdaze, and then I saw some news casts about it."

His expression changed, from alarmed to concerned. "You wouldn't be working on something related to luvdaze, would you?"

"And if I were?"

"I'd tell you to find something safer, like the heroin gangs in the slums, or sky diving without a parachute. Libby, the people involved with this thing have money, connections, and they don't mind leaving bodies."

"So you do know something about it."

He shook his head vigorously. "More than I want to, and I don't want to learn any more. Lib, I'm warning you. Whatever you're being paid, it's not worth it."

I sighed. "Paul, I'm going to send someone around to talk with you. Are you free about two tomorrow afternoon?"

His shoulders slumped. "Yeah. What are you going to look like?"

With a smile, I said, "Her name is Jasmine Keller. About my height, dark hair, kinda nerdy. She's going to want you to introduce her to people. I think she's interested in setting up a supply pipeline to Calgary."

"I hope she wears a bullet-proof corset," Paul said. He leaned forward again. "Libby, watch your damn back. I caught a couple of rumors that the money behind this thing comes from way up the line."

He walked away to take a customer's order. Paul was my main connection into Toronto's nightlife and underground. I wasn't sure if he'd know anything useful, but I was glad I'd followed that instinct. I hadn't considered that people in the corporate world were financing the drug. Criminal hierarchies could be every bit as rigid and powerful as the corporations that ran the international drug trade. Usually they stayed off each other's turf.

After finishing my beer, I took the subway across town to visit an old friend of my dad's. Dad took me to meet Vincent Overton when I was fifteen. The man was a genius, a former corporate chemist who discovered several major life-saving drugs when he worked for CanPharm Corporation, the largest pharmaceutical company in Canada. His business after retirement took a different direction.

Vincent didn't keep regular business hours, and if he had a phone number, I didn't know it. I showed up and knocked. Sometimes he answered, sometimes he didn't. If he had a client, he wouldn't answer. This time, I was in luck.

"What can I do for you, Miss Nelson?"

"I need information," I said, offering a bank card. Vincent took it and charged it a thousand creds. If I needed more information than that bought, he would simply stop talking and hold out his hand.

"I want to know about luvdaze," I said.

"I don't sell recreational drugs," he said. "Good day."

"No, you misunderstand me. I don't want the drug, I want to know about it. It appears to be very new and in a completely different chemical class than any previously known drugs. The chemical composition leads me to believe it's too complex for some kid to be whipping up batches in his garage."

A slight smile grew on his face and his eyes lit up. "You are here to purchase knowledge?"

"Yes."

For the next hour, he took me through the chemistry and what it would take to make luvdaze. The research I had done after reading Blaine's dossier turned out to be correct. It wasn't an easy drug to make, and the equipment necessary was fairly sophisticated.

Vincent seemed very pleased that I followed most of his explanation. "Do you have any more questions?"

I held out my card again. He raised his eyebrows, but took the card and scanned it, then waited expectantly.

"Who is or was pursuing research that might have led to the discovery of such a drug?" I asked. From what I'd learned already, I suspected luvdaze was a failed drug in a research line conducted by either a pharmaceutical company or university researchers working under a grant.

My question was rewarded with a big smile. "Excellent, Miss Nelson." He gave me three names— researchers in Switzerland, China and Canada.

"What is the point of the research?" I asked. "I mean, what disease or condition are they working on?"

"Von Brandt is working on schizophrenia, Ching works in sports medicine, specifically in areas of increasing stamina. Sheridan is working on enhancing female libido. All three have published papers on work they've done with compounds chemically similar

83

to luvdaze."

"Chemically similar," I repeated. "My understanding is that swapping out a benzene ring here and an aldehyde group there can get you a completely different drug with different effects. An analog of a drug that kills cancer cells may have a mode of action that blocks an environmental toxin. Is that correct?"

"Essentially. A drug may cure the disease you're targeting but cause undesirable side effects. Minor modifications may eliminate those side effects. On the other hand, a minor modification may give it lethal side effects, such as liver failure."

"But a change also may change the primary effect."

"Yes. A lot of trial and error goes into such research."

"So," I said, "luvdaze might be a failure that happens to have a recreational market."

"If I were guessing, I might come to such a conclusion," Vincent said.

"Thank you. I appreciate it." I rose to leave.

"I've enjoyed your visit, Miss Nelson. Most of my clientele is only interested in the effects and means of administration of my goods. Please, feel free to come again."

Yeah, feel free anytime I want to spend two thousand creds for a little conversation. It was money well spent, though.

CHAPTER 8

Albert Sheridan was a professor at the University of Toronto and a researcher for CanPharm. Call me lazy, but I decided to check him out first before taking trips to Switzerland and China. The chemistry in his published papers was a bit too dense for me to follow, but I could understand enough of the narrative parts of the discussion. I could also compare the chemical structures of the drugs he was working with to luvdaze.

A check on his finances showed that while he lived well, he didn't show any big spikes in income the past year or so since luvdaze hit the streets.

That research soaked up most of my Tuesday, and I needed to get ready for my date with Ron. When a girl can count her dates in the past year on her thumbs, she treats them as something special.

I washed and dried my hair, pulled out a red wrap dress with a mid-thigh hemline, and a pair of matching heels. I hesitated over jewelry. Diamonds were a little too ostentatious for a first date. I chose a three-strand necklace of turquoise beads with matching dangly earrings I'd bought in Dallas the day I followed Maria around.

Although I was tempted to ride my motorcycle, I wasn't really dressed for it, so I called a taxi, which deposited me at the restaurant at the appointed time. I opened the car door, and a hand extended toward me. Peering up, I saw Ron in a stylish black suit. I allowed him to help me. He did do romance well.

The restaurant was new to me, and so I was slightly surprised when the maître d' escorted us to an elevator. The door opened onto a covered rooftop terrace overlooking the lake. Candlelight and a fake breeze so soft the flame barely flickered. White tablecloths and fine crystal. Food almost as good as Dominik cooked. But the best part was Ron, who was witty, charming, and respectful. I discovered that in addition to motorcycles, he enjoyed rock climbing, the only outdoorsy thing I ever did. Of course, I didn't tell him that my learning to climb was to develop a professional skill.

We liked the same music, the same kind of vids, the same kind of art. If I'd been in a suspicious mood, I would have wondered if he had researched me. Since I knew exactly what information about me was available on the infonet, he couldn't have learned any of those things in advance.

Three hours later, we stood on the sidewalk and he said, "Shall I call you a taxi?"

"Did you ride your motorcycle?" I asked.

"No, I'm not exactly dressed for it."

"Why don't you call *us* a taxi."

His home, two stories and very impressive, was connected to the funeral parlor.

"Who all lives here?" I asked as he showed me in the front door. The foyer opened on a large living room to one side and a formal dining room on the other. A hallway stretched away into darkness ahead of us, and I was sure a door to our right led to the funeral home.

"Just me. My parents were killed in a plane crash six years ago. My brothers were already married and had their own homes, and since I'm the one who runs the business, I took the house."

"It seems pretty big for one person."

"It is. I have about half of it closed off."

He led me to his bedroom and lit a couple of

candles. We slowly undressed each other. I already knew his arms were covered in tattoos. They connected to an elaborate lace pattern on his chest and another one on his back.

A man who knew how to kiss was such a pleasure to find. A man who knew how to touch me was even rarer. A man who wasn't in a hurry was a treasure. Ron hit all three notes.

⊕⊕⊕

When I got home around noon the next day, I changed clothes, donned my Jasmine Keller persona, touched base with Wilbur, and took the subway to the University of Toronto. Professor Sheridan's lab in an annex of the chemistry building had security and guards. I thought that was a bit unusual. In my time at the university, I'd never seen such security. On the other hand, I didn't spend much time around corporate-funded laboratories.

If it hadn't been broad daylight, I would have bypassed their security, but climbing the walls in plain sight of the world would have probably attracted attention. Forced to be good, I called his lab and asked for an appointment. The sweet-voiced woman who answered the phone told me that would be impossible. The professor was far too busy, he never granted interviews or spoke to the press, and if I wanted to meet with him, I should wait until hell froze over. She was a bit more diplomatic than that, but I got the hint.

With my plan for the day stymied, I assumed my normal form. After stopping by the realtor's office and picking up the key, I descended into the slums to fetch Miz Rollins. The two of us, along with Nellie and her brother Tom, who insisted on coming, went to inspect the old school.

Compared to the abandoned tenement, the school was huge. Twenty-four classrooms, a half-dozen offices, a teacher's lounge with a bathroom, janitor's shop, kitchen and cafeteria, a gym with a basketball court and girls' and boys' locker rooms. Plus four other bathrooms. A fenced playground outside was mostly dirt and weeds, but it was huge.

"They only want fifty-five thousand for all of this?" Tom asked.

"The realtor said the bank just wanted to get rid of it. It's not in a neighborhood where the land is worth that much, and whoever buys it will have to tear down the school." I grinned. "I didn't tell her we weren't tearing anything down."

"It's too big," Amanda said. "What am I going to do with all this space?"

"So close off what you don't need," Nellie said. "At least here, you might get some volunteers to help you. People won't be afraid to come here like they are where you are now." She suddenly laughed and with a big smile said, "We can hold a fundraising event. I'll get the band and we'll do a show. It will raise money to clean the place up and get you some publicity."

I wasn't so sure. "You're contracted to Entertaincorp. I don't think they'll like you giving your services away."

Nellie wasn't buying it. "Oh, Richard will let us do it. It's good publicity. The PR people will contact the press. It makes the corporation look good. Just look at this playground. We could have two or three thousand people."

I left them to their planning, called Dad, and made arrangements to meet him at the realtor's office later that afternoon. Then I dropped by Mom's to check on my other charity project.

When I knocked on the kitchen door, the dishwasher answered it. Instead of the surly greeting I usually received, he turned and shouted, "Glenda, someone to see you."

My waif bounced into sight, wearing a chef's white pants with the legs rolled up, a shirt with the sleeves rolled up, an apron, and a huge knife in her hand. "Miz Libby!" she squealed and rushed toward me. I dodged.

"Glenda, be careful of that knife!"

She gawked at it as though she had no idea how it came to be in her hand, and said, "Oh, okay." With a little more deliberation, she gave me a hug. Her face had filled out a little, and she didn't seem quite so skinny. Behind her, Dominik came into sight with a soft smile on his face.

"Hey, Libby," he said. "You're distracting my helper. Glenda, I really do need the carrots and potatoes today."

"Okay, Mr. Dominik," she said, then to me, "I'm learnin ta be a prep cook. I chop up all the vegtables." She turned and went back into the kitchen.

I looked at Dominik.

"She really is a sweet kid," he said. "Smarter than I expected. Tries really hard and never complains. Lilith asked if I could find something for her to do. You know, Libby, cooking doesn't require an education beyond reading, writing, and math, and you can make a good living at it."

I gave him a quick hug and a kiss on the cheek. "Yeah, I know. Thank you." Dominik earned a six-figure salary plus his share in the restaurant's profits.

Mom knew better than let a good thing get away.

I went up to Mom's office, chatted with her a little while, and left her some money for anything Glenda might need. Such as a cook's uniform that fit.

After meeting Dad at the realtor's office, I signed the papers, made a down payment on the school, and got the utilities turned on. While I was there, I also rented a small apartment a few blocks from the university. That cost as much as the mortgage payments on the school, but Blaine would pay it.

I walked out in debt for the first time in my life. It suddenly hit me. Between the school and Glenda, I suddenly had responsibilities. Like a real adult.

I made a quick shopping trip to buy a wardrobe for Jasmine. I could image one, but since imaged clothes weren't real, they disappeared when I took them off. Such things as coats and shoes, for instance. If I was going undercover as a university student, who knew what kind of situation I might end up in. I had been a student four years earlier and hadn't forgotten what it was like. If everyone else was taking their clothes off, I'd draw the wrong kind of attention if I kept mine on.

I took my new clothes to the apartment. The place wasn't too bad. I'd been lucky, never having to live in such a place. Dad gave me the townhouse rent-free when I started university.

Breakfast at a little dive I used to go to when attending the university was still pretty good. I liked their banana-nut pancakes. I dropped by Lilith's and spent an hour with Glenda. She had her alphabet down and could sound out words.

The new orphanage had a dozen volunteers working on it. The broken windows had been replaced and the kitchen was clean. Two guys were in the process of re-wiring the large walk-in refrigerator. Small posters outside advertised a concert by Nellie and Blues Revival on the last Saturday in August.

The next night, I assumed my Jasmine Keller guise and went to the club Mark Wellington frequented. The band wasn't very good, but they tried to make up for it by being loud. It probably didn't matter since most of their clientele had the awareness of a rock. It was still early, and those who weren't already stoned were working hard on getting there.

Sipping on a beer, I played wallflower, hanging around the periphery and watching. One of the things I'd noticed before, especially since I was following Mark and Susan Wellington, was how young a lot of the kids were. Down to sixteen or even fifteen. The oldest were around my age of twenty-five, except some of the staff and a couple of men in their early thirties who tried to dress to fit in, but didn't quite make it.

I pretty much ignored those who stumbled in already high. I was interested in identifying the dealers. One of the bartenders attracted my attention right away. Three or four university-age kids were also doing business, and they were regularly visiting the two older men.

Around eleven o'clock, a girl who seemed familiar walked in. It took me a few minutes to place her. It was a face-palm moment when I did. Mark Wellington's girlfriend.

Instead of going to the bar for a drink, she headed toward one of the older men. They greeted each other and shook hands. The girl smiled and walked away and into the ladies' room. I followed her.

As I walked in, I saw her enter a stall at the far end and close the door. When she came out, I was waiting for her. Looking past her, I could see a small one-shot jet injector lying in the corner.

"Luvdaze?" I asked.

"Huh? Who are you?"

"I'm new in town, and I'm looking," I said. "Someone told me you knew the scene."

"Who told you?"

I took a chance. "Susan Wellington. Her mother knew my mom at school."

She nodded. "I'm Shannon."

"Jasmine."

"What are you looking for?"

"The best stuff. I have a friend in Calgary who can move it."

Shannon smiled. "Give me your phone."

I did and she entered her number. "Call me tomorrow."

She walked away and I shook my head. If I was that gullible, I'd have been dead before I hit eighteen.

Next, I approached the bartender who I suspected of dispensing drugs.

"A pint," I said, "and whatever the evening's special is."

He smiled. "That'll be twenty."

I pushed my card across and he scanned it on two different readers. He handed it back and I checked it. One transaction for five credits and one for fifteen. In exchange, I received a pint of beer and a plastic packet with green vegetable-like matter inside.

I gave him a wink. "Thanks."

The evening progressed and the patrons grew increasingly intoxicated. Those on luvdaze paired off and left. In fact, those who were alone and also displayed the symptoms of luvdaze use seemed very receptive to complete strangers approaching them. I wondered what users did if they were alone when the aphrodisiac effects kicked in. Shannon left with two university boys, and I wondered how badly addicted she was. Definitely living on the wild side.

As the crowd thinned out, the two older men spoke to the club manager, handed him a credit card, then left. I followed them.

As I passed the first alley, I blurred into the shadows. Just as with the reptilian chameleon, I could blend into the background when I stayed perfectly still, but when I moved, someone could see me. I couldn't adjust fast enough to match every background. Still, I was a better shadow than anyone else.

Unfortunately, I could only follow them until they got in a car and drove away, but I did get the license number.

⊕⊕⊕

The drug dealers' car was privately licensed, not a corporate vehicle, but I'd expected that. The owner lived in a lower-middle class part of town. My guess was that I'd have to go up the ladder from them to get closer to the source of the drug.

Shannon McDonald turned out to be the daughter of a middle manager at Hudson Bay Exploration. She was nineteen, two years older than Mark and Susan, and ready to start her second year at the university. Hooking the son of her father's corporate boss was a good career strategy. The girl had ambition. My brief encounter with her left me unsure about whether she had any brains.

She had told me to call her the following day, but from what I'd read, she wouldn't be awake and coherent until the day after that.

I contacted Wil, and when he came over, I handed him the drugs I'd purchased the previous evening. "Can you get this analyzed and let me know what's in it?"

He opened the packet and sniffed it. "Smells like marijuana."

"Looks like it," I said. "I want to know if it's laced with anything else and how potent it is."

He tucked the packet away.

I gave him the identity of the luvdaze dealer from the club. "Do you think the Chamber can find out who he's working for? I would assume one of the crime gangs, but I don't have any contacts in that world."

"You don't do drugs, don't know anything about criminals. Damn, girl, why did they choose you for this job?"

"I mostly work with corporate clients," I said. "Maybe Blaine is comfortable with me."

He gave me a raised eyebrow. "Maybe."

That set off some alarm bells. "He told me he didn't have any operatives young enough to fit in. He also said one of my clients recommended me."

"Well, that's probably true." Wilbur had come into the club briefly the night I met Shannon and he stuck out like a vid star at a high school dance. "Who recommended you?"

"Simon Wellington. And?"

He studied my face for a long while. I could tell his mind was working. After a while, he said, "How long have you been in the business?"

I didn't ask him what business he meant. "I started training when I was about twelve. Not formal training as such, more of an apprenticeship. My father was the head of security with a large corporation."

Nodding, he said, "That doesn't answer my question. How long have you been doing jobs for pay?"

"Since I was sixteen. Almost ten years."

"Ever have a client set you up? Hired you, but wanted you to fail?"

"In a sense. One of the services I offer is intrusion testing. For example, a museum really didn't want me to steal a valuable artifact."

"Did you manage to steal it?"

"Of course. I wanted the follow-on money for redesigning their systems." Why would Blaine want me to fail? "Ah. One of his bosses suggested me, so he had to make an effort. If I succeed, it points out a weakness in Blaine's organization. My dad said that if I failed, it wouldn't really count against my reputation, since even more experienced operatives had failed."

"But if we succeed, it will enhance both of our reputations," Wilbur said.

I grinned. "We?"

He grinned back. I so wanted to make 'we' more than professional. Even the wonderful night I'd spent with Ron didn't lessen my attraction for Wilbur. I

95

scolded myself for being greedy. I rarely had a boyfriend, and there I was fantasizing about having two.

⊕⊕⊕

I spent the rest of the afternoon in my Jasmine guise checking on student hangouts near the university. That evening, I went bar hopping. I wanted to see if other places were as immersed in the drug culture as the Drop Inn. A couple of other clubs catering to the university crowd had a lot of drugs going on, but nowhere was it as extensive and blatant as the Drop Inn.

I tried three clubs catering to a more middle-class clientele. One of them turned out to have an open drug scene, but I didn't see luvdaze in use. That made sense, as a dose of luvdaze ran a hundred credits.

Around midnight, I hit a mutie bar that I used to hang out in. I couldn't remember why I stopped, but after five minutes inside, I remembered. Lots of drugs, and luvdaze among them. Considering some of the unattractive physical mutations, I could see the appeal of an aphrodisiac drug. That gave me another idea.

The next bar I tried was a vampire hangout. As Jasmine, I fit right in. Non-vamps made up about half the patrons and were mostly girls. Maybe boys weren't into being dominated, or maybe they were less willing to admit it. The girls ranged from nerds like me to sweet church girls to goths, all lusting after a good-looking vampire to take advantage of them.

After observing the scene for a while, I realized a lot of the non-vamps were on luvdaze. I didn't see any vampires who displayed its symptoms. Further observation led me to believe it was the date rape drug

96

of choice. The last thing I would do in that bar was accept a drink from a vamp. I had thought the drug was only administered via a jet injector, but evidently it also had an effect if taken orally.

I sidled up to a table where I had seen a vampire lad drop something in a young girl's drink. About half the drink remained, but she was zoned out and making out with him. I took the glass as I walked past. Hiding it in my bag, I called Wil and left the club. He met me across the street.

"Can you get this analyzed?" I asked, handing him the glass.

"Sure. What's the scoop?"

"I think it's luvdaze. If not, it seems to have a similar effect. It's being passed as a powder in small capsules." I motioned with my head toward the club. "The vamps are using it like a date rape drug. The victims are awfully frisky, though. They aren't knocked out. Quite the opposite, in fact."

His eyebrows rose.

"The other thing is the vamps aren't using it themselves. I'd guess it's cheaper than what we've seen in the jet injectors."

"I wonder why we haven't seen it before."

"Probably because you weren't looking for it. You're only concerned about the luvdaze because it's being targeted to corporate kids."

CHAPTER 9

I called Shannon around two in the afternoon the next day and she answered right away.

"Hi, it's Jasmine. We met at the Drop Inn."

"Oh. Yeah." She didn't sound as though she remembered.

"You said you might be able to hook me up with a quantity."

"Oh. Yeah, right." She was silent for a minute. "What are you doing around six?"

"Nothing special."

"Meet me at Sluggo's. I'll introduce you to a guy I know."

I had no idea what or where Sluggo's was. I looked it up and found it was a working man's pub near the manufacturing district. Not the place corporate university girls normally hung out. The subway didn't run there. I'd either have to take a bus or ride my motorcycle. I decided on the motorcycle but changed out the license plate and parked it a block away from the bar.

I spotted Shannon as soon as I walked in. A perky young blonde girl stood out amongst working men drinking beer from the can. She was sitting with a man in a booth near the back.

I walked up and sat down next to her, across from her friend. It wasn't either of the men from the Drop Inn. Shannon introduced us. Forty years old with a five o'clock shadow and a beer gut, Fred wasn't what I expected. The men at the club wore suits and carried an air of sophistication.

"You want quantity. What kind of quantity?" he asked without preamble.

"What kind of prices?" I countered.

"Seventy-five a hundred."

I shook my head. "Too much."

He gave Shannon an exasperated glance, then turned it on me. "I thought you said you wanted quantity?"

"How much for a thousand?" I asked.

His eyebrows shot up and he straightened in his seat. "You got money for a thousand?"

"Depends on the price. I can't make anything buying at seventy-five."

"Give it to you for fifty."

We haggled for half an hour and I worked him down to thirty-five.

"Show me the money," he said.

"Show me the goods. I'm not stupid enough to carry that kind of money around." I turned to Shannon. "Where's a good place to make the exchange?"

"There's a bar across the street from the university called Domino's. This time tomorrow."

Fred nodded, so I did, too.

Shannon walked out with me. "What do you want for your cut?" I asked her.

"Five thousand or a hundred lot. If you sell nine hundred in Calgary at seventy-five a hundred, you'll almost double your money. Can I drop you any place?"

She stopped by what I recognized was her car.

"No, I have a scooter around the corner. Thanks. Let's make it a hundred doses, okay?" I didn't want to have to come up with more money.

She drove off, and I blended into the wall across the street from the bar. I waited for an hour for Fred to come out and then I followed him. To my surprise, he went to a bus stop and waited.

When he got on, I retrieved my motorcycle and followed the bus. Two transfers later, we were in a part of town I recognized, a few blocks from Miz Rollins' orphanage. I locked the motorcycle to a utility pole and prayed it would still be there when I returned.

In that part of town, I felt safer in my own form, so I changed. I was known down there, and at least some of the street people knew not to mess with me.

Fred didn't go very far. A couple of gang toughs intercepted him and escorted him about five blocks to an old tenement. Gang members, boys and girls, lounged around the outside. Fred went in and came out again half an hour later. The same two guys escorted him back toward the bus stop.

I followed them for three blocks until five gangbangers stepped into the street about thirty feet in front of me. Out of my peripheral vision, I saw movement to both sides and I could hear people behind me.

"You the one they call Miz Libby?" the largest tough asked. He was the only one old enough to need a shave.

"Who wants to know?"

"I'm Jorey. You took Glenda. She's mine and I want her back."

"Sorry. I'm afraid you'll have to get over her. She's gone."

He gave me an unhappy scowl. "That's too bad. I

was wantin her today. I guess you'll just have to do."

"I don't think so. You're not my type."

His leer told me I was his type. Female. "I wasn't askin if ya wanted to. Yur gonna find out yur everbody's type." That brought whistles, catcalls, and jeers from his buddies. The situation looked to be on the verge of getting out of hand, and the idea of being touched by any of them was enough to turn my stomach.

I took my pistol out of my bag and shot him in the chest. The guy standing next to him raised his hand so I shot him, too. The silencer made the whole scene surreal, quiet and in a type of slow motion. Whirling around, I saw that one of them had moved within a couple of yards of me. I blurred my form and took off at a run. As I passed the kid blocking my way, I struck him in the throat with the edge of my hand.

Whether it was the death of their leader or my subsequent actions, I seemed to confuse the other gang members because no one followed me. Or maybe they had to hold a meeting to choose a new leader. In any case, they looked around for someone to tell them what to do, and since no one stepped forward, they did nothing.

I uttered my second prayer of the day when I reached my motorcycle and found it intact. I got on and fired it up. As I rode away, I cursed my luck. I'd hoped to waylay Fred and take the drugs. Instead, I'd have to come up with the money to pay him. At least I knew where he'd gone to make his buy. I wasn't sure how that was going to help me, though.

I called Wilbur as soon as I got back to Jasmine's apartment, and he came five minutes later. The first thing he said was, "Are you all right?"

"Yeah. Why shouldn't I be?"

He gave me one of those quizzical raised-eyebrow looks. "You just had a run-in with a gang and killed two people."

"Oh, that. Jorey had it coming. That's not why I called you." His eyebrows shot up but I ignored his reaction. He'd have done the same thing. You didn't wander around in places like that unless you were either prepared or stupid.

After listening to an account of my afternoon, he said, "I don't understand the problem. You planned on ripping this Fred guy off for the drugs. What's changed?"

"I planned on getting the drugs before our meeting tomorrow," I explained. "That way I wouldn't have to pay for them. I can't rob him with Shannon there. I may need her in the future."

"Why is she going to be there?"

"Duh. She wants her payoff for setting up the deal. Do you think she trusts a person she just met from out of town to hunt her down and pay her five grand?"

He rubbed his chin. "I guess not."

"Right. So, I need thirty-five thousand from Blaine."

"Oh, is that all? That shouldn't be a problem." He pulled out his phone as I stared at him. The ease with which corporate types tossed money around always appalled me.

He wandered off into the bathroom, and when he came back he said, "Done. He transferred it to Jasmine's account. He said he'll recover the money after your meeting."

I had a card with Jasmine's name, but I hadn't used it for more than a couple of drinks. As for Fred, Blaine evidently felt the man had served his purpose.

"Wil, I'm willing to bet that Fred didn't pay for those drugs up front. If he doesn't turn up with the money, someone's going to be upset."

Wilbur chuckled and said, "We'll put that place under surveillance. It might get interesting."

I assumed he meant electronic surveillance. If you had the resources, and Blaine did, you could drop a dozen drones on the rooftops around the drug house and follow anyone leaving.

"It definitely will if the gang didn't pay up front. We're talking some large numbers for a gang living in the slums."

⊕⊕⊕

I met Shannon the next day and we waited for Fred. She seemed anxious and nervous, and I wondered if I should be also.

"Is there a problem?" I asked.

"Huh? Oh, no. I just have someplace I need to be," she said. "How much do you like to do it?"

It took me a second to figure out what she meant, but I had worked out an answer in advance. "I've only done it a couple of times with my boyfriend. I don't think I'd want to if he wasn't around."

"Yeah, I can see that."

"Mark's your boyfriend?"

"Used to be. His parents are a problem. They've stuck him in some rehab center."

103

"So who do you do it with?"

She grinned. "Whoever I want. Sometimes I just pick a guy that looks good."

"Did you ever do it alone?" I asked. "You know, without being with a guy?"

"Oh, hell no. That would be a real drag. I can't even imagine it."

Interesting.

Fred showed up. He handed me a box wrapped in brown paper and said, "Take it to the head and check it out."

In the ladies' room, I went in a stall and opened the box. The jet injectors were packaged in clear plastic clamshells with ten in a package. Each clamshell was about the size of my hand. Very professional, very corporate. I had checked, and a one-use jet injector ran about two creds if bought in bulk. The drug maker then filled them with a dose of liquid drug and sealed them. And if you were producing something for sale in a store, you probably put them in a plastic clamshell.

What basement chemist had a machine for making plastic clamshells? The whole thing stank of some pharmaceutical corporation selling drugs out the back door. Or at least some rogue employees.

I counted a hundred clamshells, then put ninety of them back in the box and rewrapped the paper around it. The other ten I put in my bag.

When I sat down at the table with Fred and Shannon, I nodded and pushed a card across the table. He scanned it and gave me a satisfied smile.

"Nice doing business with you," he said. "Come back and see me next time you're in town."

We watched him go out the door.

"Do you have your car?" I asked Shannon.

"Yeah."

"Let's go out there and I'll give you your cut."

We sat in her car and I pulled the ten clamshells out of my bag. "Thanks. I probably won't be back in town until the end of the semester, but I'll give you a call."

"No problem. You'll be the hit of the party." She smiled as I got out of her car.

⊕⊕⊕

Wil was waiting for me at Jasmine's apartment.

"You were right," he said as I opened the door. "Fred headed straight toward the place where he got the drugs. He had siphoned off five grand from that card you gave him, so I assume the rest was to pay his supplier."

"You've already taken him in?"

"Yeah. He's headed for interrogation as we speak."

I opened the box and let him see what was inside. He stared at the neatly packaged jet injectors for a while, then his eyes rose to mine.

"You gotta be kidding me," he said.

"Rather professional, don't you think? Most small dealers are going to buy multiples of ten, take them out of the packaging, and sell them as singles. I never saw any packaging like this in the clubs. But Shannon didn't blink an eye."

Wilbur pursed his mouth like he'd tasted something bitter. "I have a feeling that girl isn't paying money for a lot of her drugs. Did Fred look like a drug user to you?"

"No, not at all."

"Did he look like someone who liked hot young girls?

"Oh, yeah. You're probably right. I have no idea how he got into this sort of thing, though. The guys I see selling at the clubs are younger, more sophisticated."

Wil chuckled. "That license number you gave me? We've identified him as a mobster with the Donofrio family. He works for Fred's brother-in-law." Alonzo Donofrio was head of the largest criminal enterprise in the city.

"Shannon knows both of them," I said.

"I wonder who else she knows?" Wil mused. "And why she's going to Fred for the quantity rather than the guy who's in the scene? That doesn't make any sense."

"The mob link is worrisome, but as far as I know, Alonzo Donofrio isn't in the drug business. Probably lower level guys freelancing. What doesn't make any sense is how Fred is connected to a gang in the slum," I said. "It seems these drugs are taking a roundabout route from fancy manufacturer to fancy consumer."

"What doesn't make any sense is this packaging," Wil said. "I've seen everything from cocaine to heroin to weed to LSD to dozens of designer drugs. No one goes to this kind of trouble for street drugs."

"Kinda my thought also. Do you want to take these in to Blaine? Just leave me a ten-pack in case I need it for something." I stashed the drugs in the refrigerator. When I walked back into the living room, I asked, "Did the results come back from that drink I gave you at the vampire bar?"

"I almost forgot. Yes. It appears to be an analog of

luvdaze. The concentration of the drug in that drink was about ten times more than what we're finding in the jet injectors."

"Weaker, so they have to use more of it, but also a different method of delivery. I wonder if it's as dangerous. Hey, I'm hungry. Want to grab something to eat?"

We went to a Korean place down the street. About the time our food came, Wil got a call.

"Someone showed up at that tenement where Fred got the drugs," he said after hanging up. "We don't know who it is, but the place erupted like shoving a stick in an anthill. He left, and we're following him. Eat up and let's see what's going on."

After wolfing down half of my dinner, we trotted back to Jasmine's place and jumped into Wil's car. Nice ride, an expensive hybrid hydrogen-electric European sports car that cost more than most people's annual salaries. I reassessed where he sat in the corporate hierarchy.

"What makes you think this guy is something special?" I asked as he drove. "Maybe they followed Fred and saw him get picked up."

"He was wearing a suit," Wil said.

That certainly didn't sound like any gangbanger I knew.

"You following him with a drone?"

Wil gave me a sharp glance then turned his attention back to the road. "You sure know a lot for an indie."

"Reading is still free," I said. "All it takes is a connection. Or would you be more comfortable if I was a conventional empty-headed female?" We were driving in a nice residential neighborhood, a long way from the slum where Fred bought the drugs.

He laughed. "My mother is a university professor and my sister is a research physicist. Find someone else if you want to sell the woman as intellectually inferior shtick."

"You're the underachiever in the family, huh?"

His jaw tightened. I'd just pushed one of his buttons. He didn't respond, though.

Wil turned a corner, then abruptly pulled over to the curb.

"What's going on?" I asked.

He held up his hand, and I could tell he was listening to someone on his earpiece. After a couple of minutes, he turned his eyes toward me and said, "The guy we've been following entered a house a few blocks from here. We've identified him as a cousin of Alonzo Donofrio."

"Well, that takes a little mystery out of things, doesn't it?" I said. "I think I need to talk to Blaine about hazard pay."

"You're already charging a risk premium," Wil said.

"Yeah, but I thought I was dealing with crazed druggies and gangbangers, not the mob. Some of those guys can shoot straight."

He snorted, caught himself, then gave it up and grinned at me. "You're something else, you know that?"

"Of course I know that. You're slow."

He chuckled.

Wil might have thought I was joking, but I wasn't. I'd done a couple of jobs for Alonzo, including taking out his son-in-law. I wanted no part of anything he might view as disloyalty. Getting caught between the

Chamber and the mob was my worst nightmare.

"So now what?" I asked.

"We put a couple of men on him and hope he leads us to something. You're right; this isn't what we hired you for."

I breathed a sigh of relief as he drove me home.

⊕⊕⊕

CHAPTER 10

Ron and I had made plans for his Tuesday-Wednesday weekend. I rode my motorcycle over to his place early on Tuesday morning, and he joined me on his motorcycle. It had been a while since I had taken a road trip, and heading out on the highway felt great. Except for business, I hadn't been out of Toronto in more than two years.

He made reservations at an inn in Lion's Head, a resort town on the Bruce Peninsula that formed Georgian Bay by jutting out into Lake Huron.

The Niagara Escarpment ran through the middle of the Great Lakes region, outlining the farthest southern reach of the glaciers from the last ice age. Its most famous point was Niagara Falls, where Lake Erie dumped into Lake Ontario. But the escarpment ran from the southern rim of Lake Ontario, then north through the peninsula, and west in an arc along the western edge of Lake Michigan.

And why was that important? Because the glaciers had left hundreds of miles of cliffs and some of the best rock climbing in North America.

We rode out of town past miles of greenhouses and factories that produced and processed most of the food for the city. The upper classes ate real food trucked or flown in from farming regions around the world, but the middle and lower classes couldn't afford that. I knew people who had never tasted meat.

The three-hour ride was too short. I'd forgotten what blue skies looked like. One of the first things we noticed was that people in Lion's Head didn't wear filter masks. The air was actually that good. We checked in and grabbed some lunch, then took off for the cliffs.

The view of the lake, its crystal-clear waters, and the forested shores beyond were breathtaking. An unusual thing about climbing on the peninsula was that we started on the top. First, we had to rappel down, then we would climb back up. We secured our ropes and equipment, and made ready for the descent. Ron told me he was an experienced climber, and even though I had no reason not to believe him, I was still a little concerned. Men sometimes bragged when it wasn't appropriate.

We launched off and down the cliff in parallel. It wasn't a race, and I really wasn't in a hurry to get down. I spent a lot of time just admiring the scenery. Ron was waiting for me at the bottom.

"Have you climbed this route before?" he asked.

"Yeah, but it's been a few years."

"I'll go first, then."

Ron started up the route we'd chosen. It was tough, but not one of the hardest ones. I watched him until he was about forty or fifty feet up and started my own climb about ten feet to the right. I trusted him, but if he fell, I wanted to be out of the way.

Three hours later, I clawed my way over the edge and stood up, as tired as I'd been in a long time. It felt good. I looked around for Ron.

That's when I discovered I beat him to the top. I took a drink from my canteen and ate an apple. When he pulled himself over the edge, I laughed at him.

"I can't believe you let a girl beat you."

I was totally unprepared for his lunge. He tackled me, took me to the ground, and pinned me. I was laughing my ass off. The next thing I knew, he was stripping off my shorts. I only made a half-hearted attempt to stop him. We made love there, overlooking

Lake Huron and all the lands beyond, lying in the soft green grass on the top of the Niagara Escarpment. I had never done it outside before.

When he finished, I lay staring up at the blue sky, listening to him panting as his weight pressed down upon me. My dignity lay in tatters beside my pants and I couldn't stop smiling.

We had dinner at the inn and took a walk afterward watching the aurora borealis, the northern lights. As he tumbled me into our bed that night, I decided it was one of the best days of my life.

⊕⊕⊕

I wasn't sure what else Blaine wanted me to do, but he was still paying me. I checked on Professor Sheridan's address and found that he lived alone in the northern part of the city. His official biography said he was widowed with two grown daughters.

Without knowing his schedule, I decided the best way to get to him was to stake out his home. I rode my motorcycle out there in mid-afternoon and discovered a small park kitty-cornered across the street from his house. I could see both the front door and his garage. I sat back against the trunk of a tree, blended into the background, called up a novel on my tablet, and settled in to wait.

Sheridan showed up about six-thirty and stored his car in the garage. I waited ten minutes, then walked up to the door and rang the bell. To my surprise, a short, older woman answered the door.

"Is Albert Sheridan available?" I asked.

"No, he is not," she said, pointing to a sign by the bell that said 'No Solicitors'.

"Oh, I'm not selling anything. I was a student of his at the university."

"Then see him there." She closed the door in my face.

I walked around the corner, blurred my form, and went back, clinging to the shadows. Peeking in the windows, I found Sheridan in the dining room having dinner. His hair was thinner than in his official picture, his beard was longer, and both had more gray. He'd also put on a few pounds.

The woman didn't eat with him. She cleaned up afterward and retreated to one of the bedrooms. I waited a couple of hours while he read, then he turned out the lights and went to bed in a room at the opposite end of the house from her.

I went home to bed, then got up and came back at four in the morning. His garage door opened at seven, he backed his car out, and drove off. I followed him. He parked behind his lab at seven fifty-five.

After killing time all day, I was waiting near Sheridan's car at four forty-five.

"Doctor Sheridan?"

He turned. "Yes?"

"I was hoping I could ask you about some of your research. Specifically about a compound..." I showed him the chemical structure of luvdaze drawn out on a piece of paper.

He seemed to study it for a moment. "Who are you?"

"This drug is killing kids who are buying it in the underground market," I said. "Another analog of it is also being used as a date rape drug. I've read your papers on experiments with female libido, and the compounds you mention are similar to this. I'm hoping..."

His eyes grew round with panic, and he pulled away from me, practically trotting to his car. He jumped inside but didn't get the door shut because of my leg.

"I'm not accusing you of anything, Professor. I'm only trying to find out if this drug was part of your research, and who else might have access to your tests."

"All of my research is bounded by strict confidentiality agreements," he said, trying to pull the car door closed and push my leg out of the way simultaneously.

I didn't budge. "Professor, I'm working for the Chamber of Commerce. We are very interested in how this drug got out on the street. Are you telling me that CanPharm is selling this through unauthorized channels?"

Although the old governmental agencies and laws to control drugs were no longer in place, the pharmaceutical manufacturers had their own council with standards and procedures. The last thing any of the drug or chemical companies wanted was an infonet hysteria. Multi-billion credit lawsuits were very effective in controlling corporate behavior.

The poor man's face turned red as though he was about to have a seizure, so I relented and stepped back. "The Chamber will be taking this matter up with both CanPharm and the university."

He drove off, almost hitting another car on his way out of the parking lot.

I called Wil. "Hey, what are you doing this evening?"

"I'm at your beck and call. You know that." If he'd

put the slightest bit of purr in his voice, I would have melted, but he said it in such a dry, business-like way that it was deflating.

"Meet me at The Pinnacle at seven and I'll buy you a drink."

"I'll see you then," he said and hung up.

⊕⊕⊕

Nellie and I were having a drink while we shared a plate of poutine when Wil showed up at the club. His shadow fell across the table, and Nellie glanced up.

"Oh, my," she said. "We done died and gone to heaven. There's an angel in here."

I turned to see what she was talking about. Wil's face was so red I thought he might combust.

"Nellie, this is my friend Wilbur."

She turned back to me. "You been holdin out on me."

"Nellie, he's a sweet young thing. I've just been protecting him."

His face turned even redder.

"Wil, sit down." I indicated the chair next to me, putting him across the table from Nellie.

"You're Nellie Barton," Wilbur said. "I have all of your recordings."

She smiled and preened. "I'd be glad to give you a private concert sometime."

"Down, girl," I growled.

They both gave me startled looks. I must have put in a bit more feeling than I intended. My face felt a bit warm.

"She's doing a charity performance in three

115

weeks," I said. "Why don't you come with me?"

Nellie shot daggers from her eyes. Wil gave me a sideward look and rubbed his chin.

He looked over at Nellie and said, "I would enjoy any chance to hear one of your performances."

She smiled. It took me a moment to realize he'd said yes to both of us. He was slick and I decided to cut my losses.

Wil ordered a beer while Nellie and I finished our dinner. She gave him one of her thousand-watt smiles and wandered off. He watched her butt as she walked away.

"How long have you been friends?" Wil asked.

"A long time. Since we were little girls. Her mother used to work for my mother."

He raised an eyebrow, which told me that he knew about my mother's business. I waited, but he didn't say anything. Smart man.

"Remember when you asked me if I'd ever worked for someone who didn't want me to succeed?" I asked. His head snapped around. "Wil, I'm asking this as one professional to another. Do you have any orders specifically concerning me?"

"Only to protect you."

I searched his face, his eyes. Either he was a better liar than anyone else I'd ever met, or he was telling the truth. I decided to trust him.

"Well, let me tell you about some research I've done." I didn't mention Vincent, but I told Wil about the drug research Sheridan did for CanPharm. Then I told him about my conversation with Sheridan that afternoon.

When I finished, he shook his head. "I find it difficult to believe CanPharm sanctioned selling a

116

recreational drug this dangerous."

"Officially sanctioned, I agree. Unofficially?"

"You're thinking the board of directors has gone rogue, or just an individual?"

"Or a small group of individuals. I don't think Sheridan is in on it. I've examined his financials, and I don't see it. But someone above him? I think someone has set up a small factory."

"It would cost millions."

"I don't think so. I checked and an industrial clamshell system to do what we saw is about the size of this table and less than ten grand. Setting up a lab is fairly cheap. The chemicals and vessels to manufacture in quantity, buy jet injector dispensers in quantity, and then the packaging are the major costs. But those could easily be hidden in a research budget and then diverted."

"So you're thinking more like a hundred thousand, maybe two hundred thousand?" he asked.

"More than a meth lab, yeah. But look at the distribution profits. Wil, they're getting about twenty thousand doses per liter. On the wholesale market, I'll bet the manufacturer is getting twenty creds per dose. That's four hundred thousand a liter. No one has started cutting it yet, at least not in Toronto, but you could."

Wil sat back and blinked at me. "You're talking millions a week."

"Yeah."

"How easy is this stuff to make?"

I shook my head. "I don't know. It's a pretty complex compound, but I don't know the process. CanPharm would consider that a trade secret, so Sheridan wouldn't publish that in any of his papers."

Wil abruptly stood. "Let's go visit Sheridan."

"All right." I stood up. "He wouldn't talk to me. I couldn't even get past his bulldog of a housekeeper when I went out to his house."

His grin was rather frightening. "I think I can be a little more persuasive than you can."

We hopped in his car and headed out to North York.

When we got there, all the lights were on. Wil parked across the street, and we went up to the front door. He leaned on the doorbell for about five minutes, but no one came to answer it.

"Let me go look around," I said, stepping off the porch and heading around the corner. As soon as I was out of Wil's sight, I blurred my image into the shadows.

The first window I peered in told me something was wrong. The room was a mess, with the furniture overturned and stuff scattered about. The next room was the same. Sheridan was in his study, sitting in a chair with his back to me. The room had been torn apart, with papers scattered everywhere. I ran back to Wil.

"It looks like someone tossed the place." I passed my hand over the alarm keypad, determined it wasn't set, pulled out my lock picks, and bent down in front of the door."

"What about the alarm?" Wil asked.

"I don't think it's set."

He reached over my shoulder and turned the doorknob, then pushed the door open.

"It's not locked."

I put my lock picks away and drew my pistol. He raised an eyebrow, then pulled a hand cannon from under his jacket.

"A forty-four mag?" I asked. "You go elephant hunting in Toronto much?"

"I like the stopping power," he said and stepped into the house. Yeah, that thing would stop a medium-sized truck.

The housekeeper was in the kitchen, a neat round hole in her forehead. The back of her head decorated the stove and counter. A cold shiver passed through me. Whoever came in here played for keeps.

I found Wil in the study. Sheridan had taken one in the chest and he was already turning cold. I checked my chrono and it was about three hours since I approached him at the university.

"He made a call, either on his way home or as soon as he got here," I said. "He knew who was selling the stuff, even if he wasn't in on it."

Wil nodded. "They cleaned up this loose end fast. I'm a bit surprised that they killed the goose who laid the golden egg."

"It's not like the fashion industry," I said. "They don't need a new product every year. The drug will continue to make money forever. Besides, depending on who is behind this, they may not be in it for the long run. A one-time smash hit and then retire."

He thought about that. "It looks like a mob hit."

"Yeah, and if Donofrio is behind the drugs, then he might want to keep Sheridan alive. Relocate him, maybe. But if it's a rogue inside CanPharm, a couple of hundred mil might be enough."

A thought hit me. "Crap! Wil, we need to get to Sheridan's lab."

We rushed out of the house and jumped into Wil's car. As he gunned it down the street, I asked, "How are we going to get in there? There are guards and a security system, and the campus police. Do we need to call Blaine?"

"No, I can get in on my own authority."

"Well, that must be nice. I didn't know Chamber security agents were so special."

He glanced at me, then back at the road as he took a corner in a power slide, dodged between a car and a truck, and then gunned it onto the southbound freeway.

"I'm Deputy Director of Chamber Security for North America," he said. "I don't work for Blaine. He's local."

Oh, Lord. I had him pegged as a corporate wannabe hoping to climb the ranks to a comfortable level. Instead, he'd already hit a level where his mansion had rooms he hadn't visited in months. I studied his profile. I estimated he was around thirty-five, awfully young for such a high position. A repeat evaluation left me with the same impression. No way he was close to forty. Obviously, he was impressive in more than the looks department.

When we reached Sheridan's lab on the university campus, the place was lit up like a football stadium. We couldn't get near the lot where Sheridan usually parked his car. The press was there, shining flood lights on the area, and the lab was surrounded by yellow crime-scene tape.

Wil grabbed my arm and pulled me with him as he shouldered his way through the crowd. He showed his ID to a campus cop, and we ducked under the yellow tape.

"Be careful," the cop said as we passed. "Don't mess up the forensics boys."

Two bodies lay near the lab entrance—the security guards. The door to the lab stood wide open.

Another campus cop and a guy who identified himself as CanPharm security approached us.

"Wilbur Wilberforce, Chamber security," Wil said, holding up his ID. "This is my assistant, Elizabeth Nelson."

"We had a break-in," the CanPharm agent said. "We've got it under control."

"We've just come from Dr. Sheridan's home. He and his housekeeper are dead," Wil responded. "The Chamber is interested in what kind of research Dr. Sheridan was conducting." He gestured toward the bodies on the ground. "I'm assuming he wasn't working on improved talcum powder."

"Dr. Sheridan is working—was working—on proprietary products," the agent said, still blocking our way.

"Do I need to call Mateo Hudiburg and get him out of bed?" Wil asked, pulling out his phone. "The agreements are clear. The Chamber can investigate anything it wants to. You can guarantee I'll document any obstruction."

"Oh, no. Of course." The man backtracked so fast he almost stumbled getting out of our way. "This way." He approached one of the forensics team who handed him something. Coming back to us, he handed each of us a pair of soft paper booties. We slipped them on over our shoes.

"No one heard anything?" Wil asked.

"No reports of gunshots," the campus cop said. "The alarms never went off. We got a call about the guards about nine o'clock.

That was around the time Wil and I were at

Sheridan's house.

We wandered around, and I paid especial attention to the lab equipment. No one tried to stop me as I went from room to room. An open notebook lay on a counter. I put on latex gloves and paged through it. Someone old fashioned, who didn't dictate their notes. I slipped it into my bag.

The next room held more cops and forensics people. A woman with a blonde ponytail and wearing a white lab coat lay on the floor in a pool of blood.

"Who is that?" I asked.

"Lab assistant. Grad student named Gretchen Montoya."

"Was she the only one inside?"

The cop shook his head. Stoney-faced, he pointed to the room beyond. I went through and found two more bodies, both young. A pretty brunette and a skinny guy who still hadn't outgrown his acne, both wearing white lab coats. She had been shot in the head, and he'd taken at least two bullets in the torso.

I bent over her. The entrance hole was the same size as that in Sheridan's housekeeper.

"No one heard anything?" I asked a cop standing there.

"No reports." He pointed at a wall. "One stray shot there."

"So, at least seven shots—"

"Ten," the cop said. "The two guys outside. One took two bullets, the other one three."

I wandered back the way I'd come and found Wil in Sheridan's office. I expected the place to look like Sheridan's house, but it was remarkably clean—and empty.

"Looks as though they took everything," Wil said.

I handed him the notebook. "Usually lab notes and all experimental data are dictated. Have you found the system?"

He nodded. "Wiped clean and all the backups are gone."

"Looks like a professional hit. At least ten shots and no one heard them." His eyes darted toward my bag. He'd noticed the silencer on my pistol when I'd drawn it earlier.

"This is a dead end," he said.

"Who's Mateo Hudiburg?"

"Huh? Oh, head of CanPharm security. He lives in Ottawa."

"Good guy? Competent?"

"Yeah, Mateo's a good guy."

"This looks more and more like an inside job," I said. "Someone panicked. With CanPharm's help, we can isolate who knew about Sheridan's research, who was involved. Other scientists would have peer-reviewed his work, someone supervised this facility, someone oversaw his budget. Let's go through all those people, and we'll find out who saw gold in a failed drug prospect."

"Libby?"

"Yeah?"

"Are you any good with safes?"

My head snapped around to look at him. I must have reacted a little too much because a slight grin appeared on Wil's face. "Why?" I asked.

"Everything in here is gone, the system's wiped, and we can't find any samples of any drugs Sheridan might have been working on. All we can find are identifiable chemicals, what I assume are raw materials."

Wil led me to a coat closet next to Sheridan's office. Pushing some winter coats out of the way, he pointed.

A very thin line in the corner didn't go all the way up the wall. I knelt down and felt around. A tingle of electricity in one spot prompted me to disrupt it, and a small panel popped out of the wall. Behind the panel was the door of a safe with an electronic keypad.

I glanced up at Wil.

"Do you think you can open it?" he asked.

"Not a problem," I said, passing my hand over the keypad as I stood up and took a step backward.

He opened his mouth, then glanced down. His jaw snapped shut. "How the hell did you do that?"

I shrugged. "It wasn't locked."

He pursed his lips and stared at me. I stared back, daring him to call me a liar. Shaking his head, he knelt down and pulled a liter jar of clear liquid and another jar of white powder out of the safe. I leaned over and picked up a plastic clamshell with a couple of storage chips.

I peeked in my bag and decided it was time to do a little housekeeping. All the old tissues, napkins, dead cosmetics bottles, business cards of people I couldn't remember, and a petrified half-eaten hamburger went into a trashcan.

"This is proprietary, you know," I said, taking the jars from him and putting them in my bag. "CanPharm won't let us take them."

Wil pushed the safe door closed, and we heard it latch. He gave me a dirty look, but closed the panel over it without saying anything.

"We wouldn't dream of taking any of their property," he said, "assuming we found anything interesting."

I nodded. "Yeah, a whole lot of uninteresting around here."

⊕⊕⊕

CHAPTER 11

The sun coming through the window woke me up. That meant it was close to noon. Wil had dropped me off sometime before dawn, and I'd barely been awake enough to take off my clothes. Mercifully, I hadn't dreamed.

You'd think that seven dead bodies wouldn't bother an assassin, but none of those people did anything to deserve death. The three graduate students and the housekeeper were totally innocent. The security guards' only crime was being slow.

After breakfast, I took the two jars from my bag and put some of the contents of each into small bottles. I took a shower and got dressed, then pulled my motorcycle out of the garage.

I rode over to Vincent Overton's and parked my motorcycle in an alley a couple of blocks away. If he was surprised to see me, he hid it well.

"Come in, Miss Nelson. How may I serve you today?"

I pulled out the two bottles and handed them to him. "I'd like a chemical analysis of these. I'm assuming they are similar to the drug we discussed last time I was here."

He took the bottles and set the one with liquid aside. "What do we have here?"

"I'm not sure, but I saw a drug being used as a date rape aphrodisiac in a mutant nightclub. I had it analyzed, and it turned out to be an analog of luvdaze." I nodded at the two samples. "Those are the last things Dr. Sheridan was working on."

Vincent's brow furrowed.

"Sheridan was killed last night, and all his

research notes were stolen."

"And this powder is from Dr. Sheridan, or from the club?"

"Both of these samples came from a safe in his lab." I pulled out my tablet and showed him the chemical structure for the drug I had purloined at the mutie bar. "This was the powder from the bar."

Vincent scanned the picture to his tablet. "Come back tomorrow. After ten in the evening."

I held out my credit card and he scanned it for a thousand credits.

"That's a down payment, Miss Nelson. I don't know how extensive an analysis will be necessary."

⊕⊕⊕

I met Wil at a bar near the university. To my surprise, he suggested dinner at a very classy place.

"I'm not dressed for Maison Rive Gauche," I protested.

"Then go get dressed. I'll pick you up at six-thirty."

I have a thing for French food, so I wasn't about to turn him down. I could have a thing for him, too. That was the first time he'd suggested anything that wasn't entirely professional.

As I got dressed, I realized that I'd agreed to him picking me up. It seemed natural, since he knew where I lived, but he would be the first man ever to come to my house for a date. I'd slept with Ron, but never given him my address.

Since I didn't have to drive, or take public transportation, I went all out. A teal knee-length silk cocktail dress that did an admirable job of displaying my cleavage, such as it was. Diamond choker and earrings. I even painted my nails, such as they were. Rock and mansion climbing didn't lend themselves to long elegant nails.

Wil's reaction when I opened the door made all the effort worthwhile. His eyes popped, and his expression went blank for an instant, but he recovered quickly.

"Good evening. Could you please inform Miss Nelson that Mr. Wilberforce is here to see her?"

I smiled and struck a pose.

"My," he said, "you do clean up nicely. One might say spectacularly."

A flush of heat hit my face. "You are a flatterer."

"And you are beautiful."

I knew he was just being polite, but a four-alarm fire exploded on my face and ran all the way down to places my outfit covered.

"Be careful," I told him as I walked out and closed the door. "The last man who convinced me he meant a bunch of flowery words like that got all he could handle."

"I shall keep that in mind," he said with a grin as he opened the car door for me.

Our table was off in a private corner, and the candle in the center of the table provided most of the light. Every eye in the restaurant followed us as the maître d' showed us to our table. Wil wore an expensive dark suit cut to his figure. He was always handsome and dashing, but that night he was elegant and sophisticated as well.

Wil ordered wine, and I noticed that his French, like mine, was Quebecois, the dialect spoken in

Quebec.

"You speak very well," I said in French as we perused our menus.

He replied in the same language. "I grew up in Montreal, and went to university in France."

Glad for a chance to practice, I stayed in French. "Then perhaps I should say that you speak English very well. I've never noticed an accent."

He laughed, a sound that made me feel warm inside.

Wil was urbane, witty, and educated. His manners were impeccable. All the little things that made a man a gentleman came naturally to him. At times, I caught myself comparing him to Ron. Wil had all the polish that Ron lacked.

I asked lots of questions, and he told me about his family and his life growing up. I had learned it didn't take a lot of prodding for men to talk about themselves. In my case, the less I divulged about my family, the better.

He walked me to my door after he took me home. I unlocked it and turned around, back pressed against the door. I wanted him to kiss me, and didn't do a thing to play coy, smiling at him expectantly.

His hand stroked my cheek, and his long fingers curled behind my neck. Leaning forward, he kissed me, long, deep, and sweet. I curled my arms around him and held his head. Kind of hard to curl your fingers in someone's hair when they're shaved bald. We kissed again, and again, our chests pressed together. Heat built between us, and I felt something insistently poking me.

I broke the kiss and hugged him. We were both panting.

"I thought you had the hots for my friend Nellie," I said.

He drew back and a shadow passed briefly over his dark, sparkling eyes. His hesitation told me all I needed to know. I put a finger over his lips as he opened his mouth to speak.

"I'm not a clingy type of girl, and I'm not a paragon of monogamy myself," I said. "But know this about Nellie and me. You get one choice. There's no tasting menu, and no deciding you want the other one instead. Take me tonight, and she'll never warm your bed. Take her, and we'll be friends, but never lovers."

I smiled at him. "Figure out what you want, Wil. I'm not going anywhere." I gave him a quick kiss, then slid out of his arms, turned, opened the door, and stepped inside. Then I spun around, leaned forward, and said, "I had a wonderful evening, you incredibly sexy, wonderful man. Thank you."

I shut the door very slowly.

⊕⊕⊕

I woke in the morning from a dream that left me with an aching need. That wasn't surprising. I'd gone to bed with that same need. A long hot shower followed by a blast of cold water helped. Vindictively, I hoped that Wil was aching just as bad. Probably not. I could picture him cuddled up with some cutie he had picked up on his way home. All the man had to do was crook his finger and sort out how many women he wanted to keep.

It was Sunday, so Ron was doing funerals. I called Nellie. We met for breakfast and I told her about my date the night before.

"He is a fine lookin man," she said. "If he does come sniffin around, I'll let you know."

I smiled as I reached out to squeeze her hand. "I know you will."

After breakfast, we went over to Mom's and spent a couple of hours working with Glenda. She didn't seem interested enough in learning to read. I left her and Nellie, and went down to the kitchen. When I came back, I handed Nellie a pastry and Glenda a piece of paper. The girl eyed Nellie's pastry and the one I was eating.

"Don't I get one?"

I pointed at the paper. "Dominik said that as soon as you can read the recipe, he'll help you make your own. Until then, no pastries for Glenda."

Her eyes about bugged out of her head. "That's not fair!"

"Life's not fair, kid. I thought you had that figured out by now."

Nellie held her cherry Danish out for Glenda to take a bite, which the girl did.

"Ain't that good?" Nellie asked. "Better learn to read quick." She proceeded to eat the rest without offering any more.

The lesson went a lot better after that. By noon, Glenda was sounding out all the words and had the measurements down.

"So, you got all that?" I asked her. She nodded enthusiastically.

"Okay, scoot. Go tell Dominik you want to make pastries this afternoon."

She hugged and kissed both of us, then ran past my mother, who was standing in the doorway, and down the stairs.

"Hi, Mom. I didn't see you there."

She smiled at us. "I didn't want to interrupt the lesson. You two are going to make wonderful mothers."

"Oh, hell no. Don't even wish that on me."

Nellie laughed. "Don't wish it on no poor kids, either. I don't want no kids until I got a nanny to take care of them."

From there we went over to the school before going to dinner. Amanda and her kids had moved in as soon as the utilities were turned on. I'd offered to help, but Nellie's brother and half the neighborhood took care of it for me. Amanda showed me the fixed refrigerator full of food, and the kids' rooms with their new beds.

I started counting beds, then said, "Miz Rollins, do you have some new kids?"

"Yes, two more." She took me to meet the new additions. She also introduced me to two young women who looked like twins. "This is Dory and Cory," she said with a smile I thought would split her face. "They've volunteered to help three days a week."

We left Amanda and went to dinner at An Poteen Stil, then I took Nellie home and headed over to Vincent's, arriving exactly at ten o'clock.

Vincent welcomed me in, and I could sense a sort of excitement.

"First," he said, "the powder. It is an analog of the powder from the club. A minor difference, but I have a feeling it's closer to something that's marketable as a legitimate drug. You might find out if Sheridan put out any feelers for clinical trials."

"What kind of dosage would you suggest?"

"About fifty milligrams, I should think. The

dosage being used in the clubs is two to four times that amount. You could get a rise out of a corpse with the dosage you said they were using. Now, about the other, the liquid. It's luvdaze, pure and unadulterated."

"I wonder why he was keeping it in a hidden safe."

"You said you have a full liter of it?"

I nodded.

"Retirement plan, maybe? That's two million creds at street value. My personal opinion is you could cut it fifty percent and still charge the same amount. I doubt the users would notice the difference, and it would have a larger margin of error."

"You mean it would be safer."

"Yes."

"If that's the case, I wonder why the dealers aren't doing it. What would you cut it with?"

"Saline. Salt water." Vincent studied the analysis report on the table. "As to why? I think the people pushing this stuff are amateurs. I don't think they know anything about the illegal drug trade."

That made all kinds of sense and fit in with my theory that someone inside CanPharm had seen an opportunity and taken it.

⊕⊕⊕

I was on my way home from Vincent's and passed the Drop Inn. Out of curiosity, I pulled in for a drink. I hadn't been in there as myself since the first time I followed Mark and Susan. All my other trips had been as Jasmine.

On a Sunday night, the scene wasn't quite as loud

and raucous as during my previous visits. I got a pint at the bar, and as I turned to survey the crowd, I heard a woman scream. It was quite a scream to be heard over the band.

I drifted over that way, along with a hundred other people. Sometimes being taller than everyone else had its advantages. Standing on my tiptoes, I saw Mark Wellington's girlfriend Shannon sitting on the floor.

Making an effort to work my way through the crowd, I saw another blonde girl with her back toward me. Someone lay on the floor between the two women, and as I got closer, I could hear the other girl crying. She turned her head, and I saw it was Susan Wellington.

The body on the floor was Mark, and a bouncer was giving him CPR. Kneeling down next to him, I felt for Mark's pulse, but couldn't find one. When I peeled back an eyelid, his pupils were fully dilated and nonresponsive.

"Don't worry about it," Shannon said, her speech slurred. "He just passed out. It's happened before." She was so blasted that I wondered if she even knew which boy she was with.

Susan, on the other hand, was sobbing and pleading for someone to do something. I grabbed her arm and pulled her to her feet.

"Come with me," I said, and began dragging her toward the door.

"We can't leave Mark."

I stopped. Holding her by both shoulders, I bent over close to her face and said, "Mark is dead. What we have to do is get you out of here."

Through her shock, she managed to say, "Who are

you?"

"A friend of your mother's. Now, come on."

I couldn't see putting her on the back of my motorcycle, so I called a robotaxi and had it take her to Jasmine's apartment. Then I retrieved my motorcycle and rode over there, arriving ahead of the taxi.

I took Susan upstairs and put her in the bedroom. The Wellington's security chief's number was still in my phone so I called him.

"Mr. Fitzgerald? This is Elizabeth Nelson. I have Susan with me at an apartment near the University of Toronto. I think Mark is dead. An overdose in a club called the Drop Inn."

I gave him the address and sat with Susan until she cried herself to sleep. About an hour later, Fitzgerald showed up with Maya Wellington.

"Where is she?" Maya asked as soon as I opened the door. I pointed toward the bedroom.

"Mr. Wellington is at the hospital," Fitzgerald said. "They took Mark there."

"Did they manage to revive him?"

He shook his head. "Nice place," he said, dubiously scanning the apartment.

I smothered a laugh. "I rented it for an undercover gig. Mr. Wellington recommended my services. That was why I was in the Drop Inn. It's definitely not my usual cup of tea."

Maya came back out of the bedroom and said, "She's sleeping. Are you sure she's all right?"

"She's fine, just exhausted. I don't think she did any of the drug that killed Mark." Susan hadn't acted or looked like someone on luvdaze. I took a deep breath. "I went into the bar where I found them for a

135

drink before I went home," I said. "I don't know why, it's not one of my normal hangouts. I heard a commotion, and when I looked, I saw Shannon MacDonald. When I got closer, I saw Susan and Mark. I'm so sorry, Mrs. Wellington."

She bit her lip and glanced back toward the bedroom. Her eyes were red, and I could tell she was riding on adrenaline. I didn't have much in that apartment, but a six-pack was in the fridge and a bottle of whiskey was in the cupboard. I went and poured two fingers of the whiskey in a glass and handed it to her.

"No, no thank you," she said.

"I think you should," I told her in what I hoped was a kindly tone.

"Drink it," Fitzgerald said.

She turned her head back and forth between us, then tossed the drink back.

"Damn!" She blinked a few times, then looked around the apartment. "I guess you save your money to spend on good whiskey."

"I do, but as I was explaining to Mr. Fitzgerald, this isn't my home. I use it for work."

She sat down in a chair and said, "Thank you for getting her out of there. And thank you for calling us." Tears started running down her face.

Susan came to the bedroom door. "Mom?"

Maya turned and Susan rushed into her arms. Fitzgerald and I watched them hug and cry for a while, then I helped him to get the women down to their car.

"We appreciate your help," he said. "I'll see that something is sent for your time."

"No, that isn't why I did it. Just think kindly of me

136

if you have a chance to steer a little business my way."

His face softened a bit. "That I will. Thank you, Miss Nelson."

⊕⊕⊕

CHAPTER 12

After the carnage at Sheridan's lab, Wil evidently didn't have to work very hard to convince Mateo Hudiburg of CanPharm to give us the information we needed.

"Everything you asked for," Wil said, handing me three chips. "I have people running background checks on everyone on the list."

"Okay," I said, taking the chips. "Have them send me what they find." We'd cast a broad net, and although I felt it was important to be thorough, I planned to concentrate on people living and working in Toronto.

"Do you need anything else?" he asked. "We have state of the art facilities and the largest corporate database on the planet."

"I'll let you know." I was very aware of the Chamber's corporate database. I granted myself administrative privileges to it when I was eighteen. At one time, I considered appointing myself as their chief cyber security officer. That was too much like a real job, though.

Wil left and I went into the spare bedroom on the third floor, the room no one ever saw. The only private installation I'd ever seen to match it was my mother's. The server array itself took up one wall. The wall opposite had six monitors. As far as the infonet was concerned, the main firewall and router appeared to the world as being physically installed in Belarus. The only port that allowed incoming traffic showed as an address in Zimbabwe. It was a trap. Any hacker attempting to enter it unleashed a system-crashing set of self-replicating, dynamically-evolving viruses.

Mom was one of the best hackers who ever lived.

She started teaching me computers when I was three, and I had been inside almost every governmental and corporate network that mattered.

I plugged Wil's chips into an auxiliary system and scanned them, then copied the information off. No way I was going to let a chip from the Chamber touch my main systems. I read the information into a database, categorized and hashed it, and set up some basic search algorithms based on key words and limits.

While that ran, I started calling up the records of the business people involved with Sheridan's lab and checking their financial records in their bank and brokerage accounts. Follow the money was an old adage, and in the luvdaze case, it was the most important one. Since the elimination of currencies, bank credit was the only accepted means of exchange, and tracking money had become much easier if you had access.

During my Economic History course at the university, I thought it was funny that governments allowed the banks to crash the world economy repeatedly. Once the corporations took over, that stopped. The corps weren't about to do business with a bank that disrupted business.

One person popped immediately, the CanPharm accountant who tracked the lab's budget. Her total income exceeded her salary by a factor of five, and she was spreading it around to different banks. I spent over an hour following her funds' flows before deciding she was a false positive.

As best as I could determine, she was sleeping with a guy in the mergers and acquisitions department of a large bank, and she was trading stocks based on inside information. She was a perfect target for blackmail, since the stock exchanges frowned on that sort of thing. Blackmail is such a nasty business, though. You really have to get off on someone's fear and suffering to be successful at it. Instead, I bookmarked her brokerage accounts, analyzed her recent trades, and bought five thousand shares of a mining corporation and a thousand shares of a lingerie company.

That diversion completed, I went back to hunting inside CanPharm. One minor executive had a gambling problem, but beginning about a year before, he managed to get his debts under control. Another manager had bought his mistress a pricey condo near the waterfront six months earlier. A procurement manager bought a new house in one of the nicest parts of town, something he couldn't afford on his salary. The facility manager for the laboratory bought a couple of fancy new cars and started taking some fancy vacations.

Although the total of that money was significant, it was a fraction of the cash flow I estimated from the luvdaze traffic. I switched to checking the people involved in quality control and clinical trials.

Where would you find people to test an aphrodisiac? The next thing I knew, I was staring at a picture of a gynecologist who specialized in female sexual dysfunction. The light went on, and I wondered how dense I could be. Dr. Diane Sheridan should have been a no-brainer. Who sparked her brother's interest in his particular line of research? Perhaps his sister, who showed a long-term income in the high six figures, had convinced him there was money in women's orgasms.

Her income had skyrocketed over the past few months, and some of it had funneled into a Swiss account in her brother's name. Jackpot. I had the brains behind the scheme. I still didn't have the person who set it all up.

My smug self-satisfaction gave way to an obvious conclusion—Diane had to be scared spitless. I checked to see if she had booked a plane or train ticket out of town. Sure enough. I called Wil.

"Hey, pretty lady. What's up?"

"Wil, I know who is behind this, and I think she needs protection. Pick me up and come armed. Right now."

I hung up. We didn't have time to discuss things. I could explain in the car.

Opening the concealed vault in the other third-floor bedroom, I pulled out a submachine gun and a handful of ammunition clips. Considering the selection of potential mayhem, I added half a dozen various types of grenades. Given the level of violence at Sheridan's house and his lab, I wasn't going into a confrontation under armed.

I started out the door, but stopped. Looking at the firepower I was taking, I could almost feel my father getting ready to slap me up the side of the head.

Returning to my bedroom, I dug out of the back of my closet my bulletproof over-bust corset made of Kevlar and covered with ballistic cloth. It was very pretty, black with red piping and bows, and it definitely enhanced my figure, but it was also incredibly stiff and uncomfortable.

Wil pulled up in front of my house, and I jumped into his car, still tucking in my shirt tail. "Pearson airport," I said as I fastened my seat belt. "Sheridan has a sister, and I'm betting she's the brains behind the operation."

He pulled a squealing U-turn and blasted off

down the street. I pulled out my tablet and brought up Diane's picture to show him. She was fifteen years younger than her brother, and the picture showed her in a business suit, with styled blonde-streaked brown hair. She was pretty, but more than that, she projected an air of professional competence. I wouldn't have been surprised to see her in a corporate boardroom.

I filled him in on what I'd learned.

"Where is she flying?" he asked.

"Vancouver. She owns a vacation home on Vancouver Island." When the ice melted and the oceans rose, many of the coastal cities disappeared. Vancouver City was surrounded by hills, and the city migrated up. The ultimate result was an archipelago of islands like San Francisco, Seattle, and Montreal.

"When is her flight?"

"We have two hours."

Wil got on his phone and alerted airport security. I kept running scenarios in my mind. The two places I would target would be the check-in and the security screening lines. The safest place for an assassin to hit would be the check-in area, but I hadn't researched her habits and didn't know if she normally checked her luggage. Everyone had to go through security. Nuking the Middle East hadn't eliminated all the crazies, and every so often, some nut would try to blow himself up on a plane.

I mentioned all that to Wil, who said, "The big problem is, we don't know who might be targeting her."

"The people who took out Sheridan and the lab were disciplined," I said. "That makes me think they weren't gangbangers."

"So, any normal looking people could be mass

142

murderers."

"That's about right, but mobsters tend to dress nicely. Think tailored suits, not golf casual. Someone dressed like you are probably doesn't fit the profile."

Airport security put a hold on Diane's ticket. She hadn't shown up yet, but they would notify us if she did show up at check-in or the security checkpoint. We set up on either side of the security line and waited. It was half an hour until her flight boarded, so she didn't have much time.

"Wil," I said into my comm link with him, "I've spotted two guys from the Donofrio organization. They aren't flying, just standing around watching people like we are. One on my side of the line, one on your side." I recognized both of them. The dark glasses they were wearing inside the terminal weren't very good disguises.

I waited, but didn't get a response. "Wil?"

"Yeah, I'm here. I'm thinking."

After a while, he said, "We don't know that they're here for the same reason we are."

Even though he couldn't see me, I rolled my eyes. "Yeah, I'm willing to bet my life on a coincidence. How old are you?"

"What do you propose we do?"

"I could take them both out. There may be more, but at least that would even our odds."

Silence again. I chewed on the inside of my cheek and wondered if one sentence had blown my chances with Wil.

"What's the downside?" his answer finally came.

"Someone might see me. No matter how careful you are, chance can always screw you up. In that case, I'd have to run and you'd be here alone."

Silence again. While he thought, I edged closer to the nearest of the mob enforcers.

"Do it."

I fell against a woman, knocking her off balance. She dropped her cat carrier and lurched into the hitman. He stumbled back into me, and I slid a stiletto between his ribs next to his spine. A small push sent him staggering forward, and I moved away from the scene.

The other man was craning his neck, trying to see what was causing the commotion thirty feet away from him. I circled wide around the back of the security line, passing behind both him and Wil, then doubled back. I brushed against my target, pushed the muzzle of my silenced pistol into his side under his arm, and pulled the trigger. I didn't slow down or break stride as I walked to the back of the line, scanning for Diane as well as for anyone watching me. Everyone's attention was on the two men falling down.

I kept waiting for a comment from Wil, but he was quiet. I hadn't thought about it before, but the ability to kill quickly and silently probably wasn't the sexiest thing a girl could use to attract men.

I noticed three men in the crowd who seemed to be especially concerned about the dead men.

"Wil, I've spotted three more of Donofrio's men. One is bent over the guy near you, the others are freaking out on the other side of the security line."

"I see them."

Well, at least he was still speaking to me.

Diane's plane took off half an hour late, but she wasn't on it. We had airport security intercept the three mob guys, who were detained for bringing weapons into the terminal. Everyone seemed confused about how two men were murdered in the middle of a crowd, and Wil suggested those armed men might have had something to do with it.

Wil distributed Diane's picture and asked security at the airport and at the train station to keep a watch out for her.

As we walked out of the terminal, I said, "You might take pictures of the mob guys and try to find out who in Donofrio's organization they report to. This mess is not Alonzo's style. He's a lot more low-key and patient than this."

He pulled out his phone and gave orders. We got in the car and he pulled away from the curb. I kept waiting, but he still hadn't said anything to me.

"Wil?" I put a note of pleading in my voice. "Are you talking to me?"

"You know, it's one thing to be told someone is an assassin, but it's completely different to see her in action."

"Tell me you've never hired an assassin. Tell me you've never ordered a hit." I doubted there was a corporate security head in the world whose hands were clean. It was the way business was done, and had been done for hundreds of years. At least we didn't have wars anymore.

"Yeah, I've done it," he said.

We drove in silence back into Toronto. When we got to my place, I got out, then stuck my head back into the car. "At least I saved you from sleeping with me. You should thank me for that."

I turned and ran up the steps. It was hard keying the locks with tears clouding my eyes. I heard Wil call my name.

Just as I finally got the door open, arms circled me and pulled me against a rock-solid chest. Wil's voice murmured in my ear.

"Libby, I'm sorry. I'm such a jerk. Please, please forgive me."

I struggled, trying to get free, but unless I was willing to hurt him, he was too strong. I hated myself as I let a sob escape.

He spun me around without letting go of me, put his hand under my chin, lifted it, and kissed me.

I bit the son of a bitch. Not hard enough to draw blood, but hard enough to hurt. "You bastard. What kind of game are you playing?"

His eyes blazed as he drew his head back. I braced for him to hit me. Instead, he lifted me off the floor and carried me into the house, kicking the door closed behind us.

My back slammed against the wall, forcing my breath from my lungs. His mouth was on mine again, and his hands were all over me. He was like a force of nature, and I couldn't stop kissing him. I felt my pants slide down my legs and reached for his belt buckle.

"Condom?" I gasped.

He pulled his head back and stared at me.

"You don't have a condom?" I asked, feeling the frantic lust drain out of me.

He shook his head and his eyes rolled up, toward the second floor and my bedroom. "Don't you?"

"No." I reached down and snagged the waistband of my pants with one hand.

"You're not very prepared."

"I could say the same about you," I snapped. "I wasn't the one who started it."

146

His large hand engulfed my chin and jaw, pulling me up into a kiss. When he let me go, he said, "I'll be better prepared next time."

I pulled my pants up and shook free of him. "What about Nellie?"

He grabbed me from behind, his hands on my breasts, and pulled me against him. His breath tickled the side of my neck. "She's a nice girl. You're more my type. What the hell kind of bra are you wearing?"

I relaxed against him and said, "Are you saying I'm not a nice girl?"

He nipped my neck and let me go. Backing away, he said, "I'll be more prepared next time."

"Who says there will be a next time? What makes you think I like being mauled?"

His grin was my answer. He opened the door and left.

The adrenaline I was riding turned into the shakes, and I slid down the wall to sit on the floor. If I told Nellie about it, she'd kick my ass. Maybe, I thought, I should buy some condoms.

CHAPTER 13

Ron called that night asking if I wanted to take a road trip up to Montreal for his weekend. I told him I had to work, but he did talk me into dinner and a concert Tuesday evening. To give myself an out, I said it was tentative, and I'd call if I had to work late.

As much as Wil got me going, I considered Ron a safer choice. Stable job, always going to be there, and he treated me well. Even though he was nice to look at, I didn't feel as though I was competing with every woman in the room when I was with him. Some women are crazy. I could imagine some witch trying to take me out hoping to get her chance with Wil.

Being with Wil was like playing with a live volcano. He'd shown his volatility the evening before. I wasn't afraid he'd get violent, but we could easily push each other past limits I wasn't sure I was comfortable passing. I'd never been into pain, but I discovered bruises that morning I didn't remember getting. Some of them were due to being manhandled with that super-stiff corset on, but not all of them.

My thoughts turned to Diane Sheridan. I figured the woman was smart. If she made that plane reservation as a diversion, she was really smart. I wondered if she hung back and watched that fiasco at the airport, or if she was heading in a completely different direction under an assumed name while I danced with the mob assassins.

I rode up to her house in York, a considerably nicer neighborhood than where her brother lived. It didn't appear anyone was home, but I expected that. She lived near a golf course, and the homes were nestled into the woods. I slipped into the trees, blurred my image, and approached her property. A

148

car with two men in it was parked down the street, but they didn't see me.

My townhouse was too large for one person, and her house was easily three times as large. I wondered if she used the pool in the backyard, or if it was there for looks.

I scouted the place, disabled the alarm system, then drew my pistol, picked the backdoor lock, and entered the house. After searching all the rooms, it became evident to me that she had packed for a trip. In the master bedroom, some clothes were lying out on the bed, and an empty suitcase stood by the door. A closet in one of the spare bedrooms had luggage in it, with room for additional suitcases that weren't there.

The computer in her study was password protected. I shut it down, opened the computer's case, replaced a chip with one of mine, then booted it up again. I found her bank account records, including a couple of accounts under pseudonyms I hadn't found before. One of them was the funnel for the funds coming in. I traced it back and decided the source was another fake. Someone did a good job setting that up.

Otherwise, her email was clean. I didn't find any spreadsheets or accounts that kept track of her finances. It didn't appear she used the computer much. Out of curiosity, I clicked on a vid file.

I recognized her bedroom immediately. Oh, my. I wouldn't have thought the good doctor would have a camera in her bedroom.

Leaving the computer, I ran up to her bedroom and searched until I found the two cameras installed there. I pulled the storage chips out of the cameras and took them downstairs.

Back at the computer, I plugged in the chips and

transferred their files, then I started watching the vids again.

At first, I was interested in her partner, but after a while, I started paying attention to their conversation. I checked the file length, and realized the vid was hours long. Diane and her friend were using luvdaze. Altogether, she had thirty-two vid files on the computer, plus the two I retrieved from her bedroom. A quick examination revealed that except for two vids, they all starred the same guy.

The two exceptions were interesting. One guy with a white Mohawk looked like one of the gangbangers I'd seen through the drone camera at the place where Fred bought the drugs for me when I played Jasmine. The other guy was the only one in the vids who insisted on turning out the lights. I guessed he must have been shy, or he suspected the cameras.

The filenames were curious. The dates I understood. Something tickled at the back of my mind, and I opened my bag to find the notebook I took from the lab. When I compared the dates in the notebook to the dates on the vid files, I realized Diane and her beau had been testing her brother's creations. The filenames were comprised of dates, batch numbers, and dosages. Interesting.

Checking the files I retrieved from the cameras, I realized she was editing the vid from the two cameras to create her final files. Different people had different pleasures, but watching myself roll around naked had never appealed to me.

I didn't recognize the man. Diane was forty, and he was around the same age. I knew from her public records she was five feet five inches tall. In the nude, her body looked as though she worked out or used that swimming pool. He was a head taller and in

150

decent shape, rather handsome with collar-length blond hair. It might have been the drugs, but he certainly had stamina.

I downloaded everything from her computer, including the vids, to a chip and put it in my bag, then checked out the rest of the house.

Official records showed she owned two cars. I found the sports car in the garage, but the four-wheel-drive was missing. I even did a quick tour of the backyard, seeking a fresh grave, but found nothing. In spite of all the effort, the whereabouts of Diane Sheridan eluded me. I couldn't find a single clue as to where she might have gone. Other than Vancouver, her vacations and other trips over the past few years had been all over the world, and never to the same place twice.

Getting ready to go, I saw that the car parked down the street was still there. I went out the back door, rearmed the alarm, and retrieved my motorcycle. As I rode past, I took a picture of the car's license plate, then I went home.

⊕⊕⊕

The Chamber's database gave me the owner of the car sitting at Diane Sheridan's house, and also told me he worked for one of Alonzo Donofrio's businesses. Wil had left a message that the dead men at the airport worked for the same Donofrio business. The manager of the business was Alonzo's wife's cousin, the same one identified by the drone video at the gangbanger drug house.

That tied everything up in a nice, neat package. The only problem was that the package didn't connect to anything. I still didn't have the lab, the kingpin, or the distribution network. I had the people with the original idea, one of whom was dead and the other was on the run. I had Fred the schlub and Shannon the druggie sex fiend. I had one tiny branch of the mob.

I couldn't paint a picture. I couldn't even figure out where all the puzzle pieces fit, and the drugs continued to flow.

So, I did what I could. I took a shower and dressed to meet Ron. It took more than makeup to hide the bruises Wil had left on my jaw and my lips. I hated using illusion when I might be staying at Ron's overnight. The illusions didn't hold when I fell asleep.

⊕⊕⊕

"What kind of job are you working on?" Ron asked as soon as we sat down.

I opened my menu and thought about his question. I was a good liar, but I tried to avoid telling lies by avoiding certain topics, such as my work.

"It's a contract for the Chamber of Commerce."

"Doing what?"

I caught myself grinding my teeth, lowered my menu, and asked, "Where's the waiter? I'm thirsty."

"He's coming. You didn't answer my question."

"It's an investigation. I can't really get into it. Client confidentiality."

"Oh."

The waiter came and we ordered a bottle of wine. I was ready to order dinner, but Ron wasn't.

"What kind of investigations do you do? I don't mean right now, but in general. You said you do security assessments, but you didn't say anything about investigations."

I put my menu down and caught his eyes. "Ron, I don't mean to be crabby, but I like going out with you because it takes my mind off work. I had a frustrating, unproductive day, and I'd prefer not to think about it, or talk about it."

"Oh. Okay."

The rest of the evening went that way, with him irritating the hell out of me, turning me into a real bitch. The concert didn't help. The music was great—very soothing and relaxing—and I fell asleep. That precipitated an argument, of course.

That was why it surprised me that he wanted me to go home with him. Feeling a little guilty for ruining his evening, I agreed. That was a mistake. When I kissed him, I discovered the bruising of my lips had a functional disadvantage as well as a cosmetic one.

For the first time, I didn't stay the night. I told him I had an early meeting and took off as soon as I could.

⊕⊕⊕

I dreamed I was running through the airport. The entire place was empty, but someone was chasing me. I had my pistol in my hand, and men in suits and dark glasses kept jumping out of the cross corridors, stepping through doors, or appearing in one of the vacant shops, and aiming silenced pistols at me. I shot each of them first, but I kept expecting to feel a bullet from one I didn't see in time. The whole dream felt like being trapped inside a video game.

I woke up sweating and realized I'd forgotten to

turn on the air conditioning when I came home and fell into bed. As hot as my bedroom was, I didn't think it had anything to do with dreaming about the men at the airport. I never had such dreams, not even after my first kill.

As I ate breakfast, I realized what bothered me, what caused the dreams. It wasn't guilt, it was fear. I'd taken out two of Alonzo's boys. I didn't think anyone could ever tie me to them, but my investigation of luvdaze seemed to be going down a path that led to the Donofrio family. Before I took any more steps in that direction, I decided I should check my footing.

"Dad?" I said when he answered the phone. "I need to talk to you. Are you available this morning?"

"Sure, come on over. Have you eaten breakfast yet?"

"Yeah, just finished. About an hour?"

I showered and dressed, then walked over to his house. He was expecting me and opened the door so I didn't have to go through the full range of security unlocks.

He led me to the kitchen table and poured coffee for both of us. He gets the best coffee flown in from South America and Africa.

"So, what's the problem?" he asked.

"This Chamber investigation I'm working on. Some of the leads point to Donofrio." I told him about the murders at Sheridan's house and lab, and Alonzo's wife's cousin at the gangbanger's drug house.

He pursed his mouth and said, "And why are you coming to me, instead of taking a long vacation in Switzerland until all this blows over?"

"The whole setup feels amateurish. Vincent said the same thing when I took him some drugs to analyze. Can you imagine Alonzo using slum gangs for anything other than toilet paper?"

"Hmmm. Go on."

"I'm thinking that some of his boys got entrepreneurial on the side, and this isn't his at all. But I want to make sure before I pursue something that might clip someone close to him. Do you think you could reach out to him? Tell him I respect him and value his goodwill, and if luvdaze is one of his businesses, I'll back off."

"How will you get out of the contract with the Chamber?"

"I'll tell Blaine that he doesn't have enough money for me to go against the mob. The Chamber can do that if they want to, but I'm just an indie. I don't have any protection. If Blaine can't accept that, I can probably live with it. If Alonzo gets pissed at me, I don't think living will be one of my options."

Dad gave me one of his lopsided grins. "I'm glad you're using your head. I agree, and I doubt Blaine would push you. You've already helped him find the source of the drugs. But the hits on the professor and the lab push this thing to another level. I think the distribution of the drugs is something he can figure out without you."

"So do I, but if I'm not crossing Alonzo, I wouldn't mind getting paid as long as possible."

He laughed. "Okay, I'll go see Alonzo today. Lay low until I get back to you."

I hugged him and kissed him on the forehead. "Thanks, Dad. You're the best."

⊕⊕⊕

155

Taking Dad's advice, I spent the day on the computer and ordered a pizza online for dinner. I set up alerts on all of Diane Sheridan's accounts. She had to spend money sooner or later.

I took the clearest image I could find of the man in her sex tapes and set a match search on him in the Chamber's database.

Then I began an analysis on the distribution outside of the Toronto area. I sent Wil an email asking him to give me everything the Chamber had on luvdaze in Buffalo, Montreal, Calgary, Ottawa, Detroit, Chicago, Atlanta, and Dallas. Within an hour, he transmitted a batch of files to me.

Atlanta didn't have any information. If the drug was there, it wasn't causing enough of a problem to raise the Chamber's interest. I worked through the other cities. As I'd guessed, the closer the city was to Toronto, the earlier it reported issues with luvdaze.

Dallas was the anomaly. As far as I could tell, luvdaze hit Dallas at the same time it hit Buffalo and Ottawa. Maybe even earlier. The first reports of overdoses in Dallas showed an already thriving market for the drug. I remembered the club I'd been to in Dallas. The most recent reports were even more confusing. The supply of the drug had dried up.

The Chamber's office in Dallas had grown concerned about luvdaze just as they had in Toronto, but over the past few weeks, they reported the drug was increasingly difficult to find. In fact, the decline in supply to Dallas correlated with a rise in supply to Calgary and Edmonton, almost as though the drug was being diverted from one destination to the others.

Dad came by in the late afternoon, just before I resigned myself to ordering another pizza. He was dressed in a tailored charcoal three-piece suit and drove his power chair up the stairs onto the porch.

"Are you hungry?" he asked.

"Always. You want to go out?"

He gave me one of his teasing smiles. "As long as I'm dressed up, I thought I'd take my favorite girl out to dinner."

I raised an eyebrow. "Does that mean I should put on something more presentable?"

He took in my tank top and leggings. "If you're comfortable at The Frenchman's Daughter dressed like that, I'll take you."

"Can you wait half an hour?"

"Of course."

I ran upstairs, took a quick shower, and pulled on a dress he gave me for my birthday the year before. The halter-topped gold lamé evening gown always made me feel like I was in an old vid.

We took his car to the restaurant that billed its cuisine as 'country French'. The men in my life were treating me well. I made a note to start exercising a little more so I wouldn't have to buy new clothes.

"Did you get in to see Alonzo?" I asked after we were seated.

"Yes, and he was very curious as to why you were concerned. You know that Donofrio avoids the drug trade."

"I remember. That's why I had my suspicions some of his people were involved in this without his sanction."

"And you were right. Alonzo wanted to know if you had any names."

"Only one, and it's rather sensitive."

"Oh?"

"Jimmy Alderette." Alderette was a first cousin of Alonzo's wife.

Dad set down his wine glass and leaned back in his chair. "That is interesting. Either the young man is very entrepreneurial, or very stupid. Actually, there probably isn't a difference. If Alonzo thought Jimmy was capable, he'd give him more responsibility, where he'd earn more money." He twirled his finger, indicating that I could follow the thought to its logical conclusion, and reached for his glass again.

"Yes, well, a Chamber drone followed him from a known gang drug house. And I recognized the two men I took out at the airport from one time when I was at Alonzo's at the same time Jimmy was."

He choked on his wine. "You did what at the airport?"

"I assumed they were there to hit our mark, just as they did her brother. I want her alive so I can talk to her. So, I took care of that conflict of interest before they recognized me and things got nasty."

"Couldn't you just change your appearance?"

"In front of my contact from the Chamber? Let him know what I am?"

Dad shook his head. "My God, Libby, be careful."

"I'm trying, Dad. I can count, and there are bodies piling up all over the place. This case is as convoluted as a romance serial written by three different people."

⊕⊕⊕

We passed The Pinnacle on our way home. I was in the mood to go out and do things, but I was a bit shy about asking my father to take me to a meat market bar. Dad dropped me off at my place, and as soon as he drove off, I called a robotaxi.

As soon as I walked into the club, Paul spotted me and gave a wolf whistle.

"Wow, Libby. What's the occasion?"

"Dinner with my father. He bought me the dress, so I figure he likes seeing me in it."

"Femme fatale deluxe," Paul said. "You look great."

I hadn't really thought about it, but I was a bit overdressed for that club. To hell with it. "Give me something I'll like in a fancy glass. Might as well stoke the image."

He laughed. When he brought me a drink in a martini glass, he said, "Your boyfriend is here."

"Boyfriend?"

"The bad boy with the tats and the earring."

"Oh, Ron. Really?" A thought struck me. "Is he in here a lot?"

Paul shrugged. "Three or four nights a week."

"And he always leaves alone?"

He choked and tried to cover it up by coughing. I wasn't really sure how I felt about that. I took my drink and climbed the stairs to the mezzanine. The way I was dressed fit in better at that level. The fancy people sat up there, and an extra charge kept the riff-raff down below. Since I knew all the bouncers and didn't pay any of the entrance charges anyway, I didn't care.

I found an empty table by the railing and looked down at the crowd. Nellie was just starting a set, and she started out slow and sensual. It didn't take me long to locate Ron, dancing slow and close with a petite blonde. I could tell he had the charm turned on, and she seemed very receptive.

159

Mulling over how I felt about that, and whether I felt jealous, and whether I had any right to feel jealous, gave me something to do. I decided a little introspection was probably good. My thoughts drifted off on a tangent about whether introspection was good when I made my living doing nefarious deeds, which led to questioning whether or not Ron being a horn dog was nefarious.

A waiter came by, and I ordered another one of whatever I was drinking.

While it was nice to have a handsome guy to spend time with, and I truly enjoyed the sex with Ron, I had a hard time defining my feelings for him. I wasn't sure what love felt like, but I'd had crushes on guys in high school and university, a couple of them very intense. My heart didn't skip beats when Ron walked into the room. He was fun and comfortable.

My heart did skip beats when Wil looked at me a certain way. That scared the hell out of me.

Out of the corner of my eye, I saw the red t-shirt move toward the exit. Turning my attention in that direction, I saw Ron taking the blonde with him. I decided Mondays and Tuesdays must have been my nights. Any other time, he always pleaded that he had to work in the morning.

I suddenly realized that Ron screwing around didn't bother me. In fact, I felt a bit of relief, and that bothered me.

CHAPTER 14

When I got home, I checked the computer runs I had set. One of my computers chimed, and I examined the screen. Diane's mystery lover was Liam Campbell, head of new drug research for CanPharm. Divorced, but still living with his ex. He and his ex-wife married immediately after college, and their marriage contract was surprisingly slanted in her favor. I could see where a little extra cash would be tempting.

A check on his bank accounts was eye-popping. In a little over a year, he'd salted away over thirty million credits—three times what Diane and her brother had earned. What they were doing wasn't even illegal yet, although Wil told me luvdaze would soon be outlawed.

Some things became clearer. Still murky was the involvement with the Donofrio organization.

None of the alerts I'd set for Diane had triggered. Maybe she was hiding out in a northwoods cabin with enough supplies for the winter. I took a couple of pictures of her and set up searches in the security systems of the airport and train station. As I finished, I realized she could have driven down to Buffalo, or ferried across the lake, and caught a plane there. I set up the same search in the Buffalo and Rochester airports.

After a few minutes' thought, I duplicated the search in Detroit. That was about the farthest airport she'd be able to drive without recharging her car's batteries. And charging the batteries meant using a credit card.

The last thing I did before I went to bed was send an email to Wil asking about Fred. The Chamber had picked him up days before, but I hadn't heard anything they might have learned from him.

⊕⊕⊕

I checked my email while the coffee brewed. Wil had responded to my query.

Call me when you wake up.

I texted him. I wasn't awake enough to speak coherently. The phone rang almost immediately.

"Libby? Are you home?"

"Yeah."

"Stay there. I'll be there in a few minutes." He hung up.

I hoped he bought his own coffee. I had only made half a pot. I poured myself a cup when it was ready and popped a frozen quiche in the microwave. I only managed one bite before the doorbell rang.

"Man, are you a go-getter this morning—" I started, then the expression on Wil's face stopped me. He brushed past me, handing me a takeout cup of coffee as he passed. I closed the door, and he whirled around to face me.

"Fred Smythe is dead."

"What did they get from him before they turned him loose?" It didn't surprise me that Fred's buddies would reward him for getting caught and losing their money.

"They didn't turn him loose," Wil said. "He died in custody."

He had my attention. I inspected the coffee I held in each hand and said, "Would you like some coffee?"

"No, thanks."

I walked into the kitchen and poured the cup I had been drinking back into the pot. Then I took a sip of the mocha Wil brought me.

"Tell me about it."

Wil paced. "I was told he had a heart attack. I think that's bullshit. They're telling me that they held him for three days without questioning him, and then he died."

I headed up the stairs.

"Where are you going?" he asked.

"Need to check on some things." I heard him start up the stairs behind me.

Sliding into my chair in the computer room, I keyed in half a dozen searches as fast as I could type. I barely heard Wil's startled exclamation as he gazed around the room.

Results from a couple of the searches came back to me, and I followed them up. After about fifteen minutes, I turned back to Wil.

"Liam Campbell, Director of New Product Research for CanPharm, was Gareth Blaine's university roommate." Wil blinked at me, then his expression told me that what I'd said sank in. "Campbell is also Diane Sheridan's lover."

"Aw, crap."

"Remember when we were wondering about clinical tests? I found vids on Diane's computer of her and Campbell testing the drugs."

Wil ran his hand over his head and paced back out into the hall. "You're telling me that the Chamber's security chief is in on this thing? He's the one who hired you."

I ignored him. "There was a man in Dallas named Nikolai Sholokhov, the North American sales director for a Russian electronics control company. One of his employees named Adnan Erdowan used to make regular trips to Toronto."

"I know who Sholokhov is," Wil said.

"The drug started drying up in Dallas over the past month, starting about the same time that Sholokhov and Erdowan died. Sholokhov had a bank account that showed a number of transfers to Gareth Blaine, coinciding with Erdowan's trips to Toronto."

I turned a monitor so he could see it. "I don't think it's a coincidence that Fred Smythe is dead." The screen showed Blaine's Swiss bank account with several million credits in it.

Wil studied the two screens where I showed Blaine's bank accounts and transactions while I switched to another session and began typing again. I sensed Wil watching over my shoulder.

"What are you doing now?"

"Sending Blaine an invoice. I want to get paid before you accuse him of running a drug ring."

After reviewing the evidence I'd gathered, Wil needed little convincing. He got on the phone with his boss in Atlanta and they began pulling their agents from other cities to Toronto. At my suggestion, they avoided people from the cities with the largest luvdaze markets.

"Tell me you feel comfortable that the Chamber security agents in Dallas aren't caught up in this," I said. Wil acted like he wanted to refute my statement, but ended up just shaking his head.

We ordered Chinese takeout and ate as we brainstormed strategy. We still didn't have the two main pieces to the puzzle, the lab and the distribution chain. Wil told me the postal service, airlines, trucking companies, and the train lines were cracking down on shipping. The result was large busts of other drugs, but they hadn't intercepted a single shipment of luvdaze.

"The mob usually transports stuff in their own trucks," I said.

"Yes, I know, but Campbell and Sheridan don't have access to those trucks," Wil answered. "They're either using individuals, such as that guy Erdowan, or they have another method."

⊕⊕⊕

My phone rang a little after dark, and I saw it was Dad calling.

"Hi, what's up?" I answered cheerfully.

"A hit team is at my house," Dad said. "Watch your ass."

I heard an explosion in the background, and the phone went dead.

I leaped up and snagged my bag on my way to the door. "My dad's under attack. Time to go." The armaments I'd taken to the airport were still in my bag.

To his credit, Wil didn't ask questions or argue. When we got outside, he sprinted for his car while I opened my garage door.

"Where are you going?" he asked.

I grabbed my motorcycle and rode out, stopping by his car. "My dad's house. I'll give you a call when I can." I gunned the motor and shot off down the street. I could get there a lot faster on two wheels.

I drove down the next street over from Dad's

place and left my motorcycle under a tree. Sneaking through a couple of backyards, I peered over the fence into Dad's yard. Everything was quiet, but I could see smoke and debris near the front of his house.

Two bloody bodies lay in the backyard, both near fresh holes in the ground. I did a mental check, calling up my memory of the map of his defenses. The holes corresponded with the map. Dad had activated the land mines. I had always thought he was a little paranoid, but his maxim was 'hope for the best, but prepare for the worst.'

Blurring my form, I hopped over the fence and kept to the shadows as I made my way to the backdoor. I peered through the window and could see a gaping hole at the front of the house. I snuck around toward that side, a submachinegun in my right hand and a stun grenade in my left.

When I rounded the corner, I saw another body in the yard. Lights were on in every house on the street except Dad's. Sirens in the distance grew louder as they approached.

Something moved to my right. Looking over that way, I saw a man with a gun hiding in the neighbor's bushes. Checking my weapon, I thumbed the selector to a three-shot burst, aimed and fired. I didn't know who he was, but he had no business with a gun facing my father's home.

"Dad?" I shouted, and moved ten or fifteen feet in case someone zeroed in on the sound. Especially in the dark, I doubted anyone could spot me. I whistled a tune he taught me. His whistle answered me from inside the house.

Crawling over the rubble where a bomb had blown out the front door and foyer, I whistled again. Two more bodies lay just inside the entrance.

"Are you inside?" I heard his voice, calm and quiet.

"Yes, sir."

"Did you see any movement outside?"

"One. I doubt he was alone."

"I'm on the landing," he said.

"Okay. I'm going to crawl up the stairs."

He sat in his chair at the top of the stairs. Most people saw him and that chair and thought him a pitiable cripple. I looked at that chair and saw a tank. Swiveling machineguns mounted front and back and two rocket launchers, combined with retractable armor plating, made him the last person on earth I'd consider attacking. I never doubted my father had made enemies over the course of his life, and that chair was proof.

When I got to the top, I stood and moved to where he shielded me from any fire from the first floor.

"Man, when you piss someone off, you do a good job," I said.

"It's called the rewards of being a father," he growled. "I'm pretty sure this is a reaction to my visiting Alonzo."

"Really? Those are Donofrio men?"

"Superficially. If Alonzo wanted me out of the way, he didn't have to let me leave. I think they're people involved with your drug deal. How many bodies did you count?"

"Two down in the backyard, one in the front, the one I shot, and the two in the entrance. That's six total, but I only saw the backyard and the east side. Are you all right?"

"Yeah. I think we can stand down. It sounds like the cavalry has arrived." He was referring to the sirens that abruptly ended right outside the house. The armor plates shielding his body started retracting into the shell of the chair.

"Not necessarily," I said. "I discovered that Blaine is one of Alderette's partners. The fox in charge of the hen house hired me. Why, I don't know."

I wished I had a free hand to take notes. His profanity was always so creative.

Gunfire erupted from outside and then abruptly stopped.

We looked at each other and waited.

"Mr. Nelson? Libby?" Wil's voice came from outside.

"Come in unarmed with your hands in the air," Dad responded.

Peeking around Dad and his chair, I saw Wil pick his way carefully over the debris and bodies, his hands above his head. He looked around, and then up.

"Please identify yourself," Dad said.

"Wilbur Wilberforce, Deputy Director of Security, North American Chamber of Commerce."

Dad turned his head up to me and whispered, "You're kidding me."

"That's really his name," I said.

"His parents must have hated him." Dad raised his voice. "Is the situation outside under control?"

"I believe so," Wil said.

A new voice called from the entrance. "Jason, are you all right?"

"Yeah, I'm fine. Thanks for dropping by. I'll be down in a minute. The usual?"

I gave Dad a questioning look.

"Noah Talbot, MegaTech."

The armor retracted into the chair. Plates slid into place, hiding the machineguns and rocket tubes. Dad kept his pistol in his hand, however. He nudged the chair forward, and it tipped over the edge, riding its cushion of air down the stairs. I followed him, my weapon at the ready.

Wil and Talbot waited in the living room. Two men in MegaTech SWAT uniforms stood guard at the entrance. I hadn't seen Talbot in several years. He'd been my dad's second-in-command before Dad retired from MegaTech.

"Hello, Mr. Talbot," I said.

"Miss Nelson. You've grown up since we last saw each other."

Dad surveyed the wreckage of his home. "What a mess. The insurance company is going to have a fit."

Talbot chuckled.

Turning his chair toward the bar, Dad pulled a bottle off the shelf and set out four glasses. I felt a grin break out on my face, in spite of the tension, adrenaline, and general concern I had. That bottle had sat there all my adult life, and I'd never tasted what my father called the best whiskey in the world.

That's when I noticed the two SWAT guys were staring at me with their mouths open. I realized I had the high ground with a machinegun pointed at the room. I lowered the muzzle and saw them relax.

Dad lifted his glass, and the rest of us joined him at the bar.

"Thank you all for coming to my party," he said.

We all chuckled, clinked glasses, and tossed the two-hundred-year-old whiskey into our mouths. On first impression, it was smooth as glass on the tongue and slightly sweet. Then it turned smoky, and went down like someone turned a blowtorch on my throat. Wil and I both gasped. Dad and Talbot smiled at us.

"So, who did you piss off?" Talbot asked.

Dad turned to Wil and I. "Perhaps you'd care to explain?"

Wil glanced at me, pulled out his identification and showed it to Talbot, then said, "Mr. and Miss Nelson are assisting the Chamber with an investigation into some drug trafficking. It appears we're getting closer to some of the principals than they would like."

Talbot nodded. "Does this have something to do with the ODs I keep seeing on the newscasts?"

"That's the problem we're working on."

"Simon Wellington's son died recently," Talbot said.

Wil turned to me.

"Yes, sir," I said. "I've been working undercover, and I was there when it happened. I just found out today that the source of the drugs that killed him has also died."

"Counting the nine here, we're well into setting a record for any investigation I've been part of," Wil said. "We think these guys, or buddies of theirs, were responsible for seven deaths last week."

Another SWAT guy came in and spoke to Talbot. After a couple of minutes, Talbot turned back to us.

"We intercepted a car coming into the neighborhood. The four men inside were heavily armed, so we're detaining them for questioning. Jason, where are you spending the night?"

"My place," I said. "Go get packed, Dad."

"Are you sure that's a good idea?" Wil asked. "If they came after him here, what makes you think your place is safe?"

I shrugged. "They'd have to find it first. No one knows where I live. All my mail comes here, and Dad rents the townhouse to some guy named Noah Talbot." I winked at Talbot. "Or, at least that's what it says on the books."

"Gareth Blaine knows," Wil said.

"That's true. I forgot." I felt a little stupid for not fully considering Blaine's involvement.

Talbot's head snapped around. "What does Gareth have to do with this?"

"That's a good question," I said. "He's the one who hired me to investigate the drugs, but we think his college roommate is manufacturing it. He was also friendly with the man we think was taking the drugs into Dallas."

"Was?"

"Blaine's buddy died, and word is that the supply in Dallas is drying up."

Dad gave me a raised eyebrow, and I nodded very slightly. His eyebrows raised higher.

Talbot turned to Wil. "Perhaps you should have a conversation with Gareth."

The Chamber was powerful, but it derived its power from its members. MegaTech was one of the top fifty corporations in the world, and the largest company headquartered in Toronto. The company's chairman was Simon Wellington's neighbor.

Wil took some time to formulate his answer. "I have agents coming in from other cities, mostly from cities where luvdaze isn't a major problem. We have a major player on the run. The scientists who developed the drug are dead. Our information is that these guys," he waved his hand toward the hole where the front door used to be, "are part of the Donofrio family. My instinct is to put Blaine under surveillance, but not tip him off to our suspicions."

Talbot thought about that, then said, "Sounds like you have your hands full." He held out his business card. "If you need any help from us, let me know."

"Thanks. I appreciate that."

⊕⊕⊕

Wil and I helped Dad pack his stuff and put it in his car. Talbot posted three around-the-clock guards on the house and contacted someone to rebuild the front of the house. He also detailed three men and a couple of drones to guard my house.

My bedroom was on the first floor, so that was where I put Dad. I took the spare room, the one with the hidden arms vault. It only had a twin bed, but even if I did lose my mind and want to bring a man home, I would never do it with my father in the house.

While I might be squeamish about offending his delicate sensibilities, I discovered I was the only one in the family who felt that way. Dad called Mom to tell her he'd temporarily relocated, and she rushed over immediately.

"Jason, are you all right?" she hugged and gushed over him as soon as she walked in the door.

"Oh, yeah. I'm fine. The house is a little dinged up, but Libby came and took care of all the bad guys."

She glanced at me. "Are you all right?"

"Yeah, Mom. I'm fine."

She turned back to Dad and forgot all about me. She ended up spending the night, and I discovered the soundproofing inside the house wasn't all that great. I

172

didn't know someone in the spare room could hear people making love in my bedroom. I didn't think I was as loud as Mom. I hoped I wasn't. It was a really weird night.

CHAPTER 15

Ron called the following morning. "Hey, Libby. I miss you. Do you have any time?"

"Not really. Things are pretty crazy. My dad's place needs some renovation, so he's moved in with me for a while."

"Oh. That's a drag. Johnny Jack is playing at The Crown Royal tomorrow night, and I have tickets. I thought you might like to go."

Why would he think I wanted to see an eighty-year-old blues legend play in one of the most intimate and acoustically perfect clubs in town?

"Yes."

"Huh?"

"I said yes, I want to go."

"What about your dad?"

"Screw my dad. I can see him anytime."

Ron laughed.

When I hung up, I heard a chuckle behind me. "Who am I being dumped for?"

"Johnny Jack."

"Oh, well, I'd dump me, too." Both my and Nellie's love of blues and jazz came from my dad.

I went over to where he was staring at the inside of my near-empty refrigerator and gave him a hug. "Have Mom take you out to breakfast and buy some groceries."

"You should have had that idea fifteen minutes ago. She already left."

My doorbell rang. I peeked through the peephole and saw it was Wil. When I opened the door, all I could do was stare. He had bags of food in both hands, along with a takeout cup of coffee. Another takeout cup rim was clenched in his teeth, and it was obvious he'd spilled some maneuvering from his car to my porch.

"Wait right there," I said. "I need to go get my camera."

His eyes bulged and he opened his mouth. "Dammit, Libby..." the coffee cup in his mouth hit the floor, splashing over his shoes.

I reached out and took the other cup. "Wow. Thank you." Turning to go back in the house, I said, "Be sure to wipe your feet."

"That wasn't funny, Libby," he raged as he followed me.

His diatribe cut off when he saw my father.

"Hi, Mr. Nelson. I brought some groceries. I thought you might want some breakfast."

"Thank you, Mr. Wilberforce," Dad said. "As far as I can tell, Libby is living on a beer diet. And by the way, my name is Bouchard. Nelson is her mother."

"Beer and coffee are staples," I said. "You didn't look in the cabinet. There's some dried cereal to go with the beer."

He gave me a horrified stare.

Wil started putting the groceries away. "Since I bought the food, maybe you could fix breakfast."

"Maybe pigs will fly," I said. "There's a reason I don't buy food that needs cooking."

"I'll fix breakfast if you two get out of the way," Dad said. He took a box of eggs from Wil and put it on the counter. "You don't want Libby to cook. Assuming she doesn't burn the place down, I still wouldn't chance it being edible."

"If you had Dominik, would you cook?" I asked.

When I lived with Mom, I ate what everyone else at Lilith's ate—Dominik's cooking.

"Of course not," Dad said. "Taking food out of his hands would be a tragedy."

I went upstairs and checked my computers, hoping some of the searches I'd set up were successful. No luck, but a news alert. Fred Smythe's funeral was that afternoon. Not that it was newsworthy. The alert program had picked up his name from the funeral announcement. I started to write down the address and stopped. Calderone Funeral Home. I could find my way to Ron's.

"Libby, it's food," my dad's voice called from downstairs.

My table appeared the way Dad's always did when I visited. An omelet with bacon and biscuits, marmalade, orange juice, and more coffee.

"You're hired," I said as I sat down.

"Just show up when I'm cooking," Dad said. "You know I'll always feed you. What are you doing today?"

"Going to a funeral." I told them about Fred.

"If he's involved with Alderette," Wil said, "that could be dangerous."

"For me, maybe. I'm going as Jasmine. I need to find a new connection, after all."

Wil volunteered to send a couple of his men with me.

"You can send them, but not with me. I don't mind the protection, but I want people to think I'm alone."

⊕⊕⊕

After breakfast, I booted Wil out because I didn't need him hovering. I morphed into Jasmine, found a black dress that was out of style, and put it on over my bulletproof corset.

I parked a couple of blocks away and approached the funeral home from the side where trees shielded Ron and his neighbors from each other. Blending into the background, I watched the mourners show up. I took a picture of anyone I didn't recognize and sent it to my server.

Fred's ex-wife and a young man with a white Mohawk showed up together. The guy matched a picture taken by the drone at the drug house. He was also on one of Diane Sheridan's vids.

Soon after, Jimmy and Alice Alderette stepped out of a limousine.

As was usual for funerals, people milled around outside for a while, no one really wanting to go in. Five minutes before the starting time, they began to file inside. I stepped out of the trees onto the sidewalk and walked toward the chapel. Another limo pulled up, and Gareth Blaine got out.

I stopped in my tracks and turned away. Blaine would recognize Jasmine as me. I thought furiously. Without a mirror, I needed to use a form I was familiar with. I chuckled as I morphed my features into the rich woman I'd used when tailing Maria in Dallas. No one would suspect a woman in her fifties of being a spy.

Ron, dressed in a somber black suit, stood at the entrance to the chapel welcoming the mourners. He gave me a strange look I couldn't interpret. I signed the guest book as Winifred Parsons with my left hand as I scanned the names. Dareen Smythe was followed by Billy Smythe. That solved one mystery.

I found a seat in the last pew. As the service started, Ron came in and sat off to the side near the front. If he was doing Fred's funeral, and Alderette was related to Fred, I wondered who else I might find.

I slipped out and searched for a washroom. I saw it across the lobby, but turned away and walked down another hall. Ron had told me about the general layout of his operation. Turning a corner, I blurred my form and proceeded very slowly down the hall. Even with a security camera, it was difficult to identify my presence if I moved slowly. The electronic keypad lock on the door at the end of the hall took seconds to disable.

I passed through an area of offices and then a showroom with half a dozen caskets on display. Miz Rollins' kids never slept in beds as luxurious as those caskets. People had their priorities misplaced.

Behind all that and through another locked door was a long hallway with two doors. The one on the left opened into the room where they embalmed the bodies. All four tables were empty. The other door led to a morgue-like refrigerated room. Drawers stacked four high and eight across lined one wall. A dozen of them had tags. I opened the closest one and discovered one of the men I'd killed at the airport. The next drawer held the other man.

I checked the others and found Professor Sheridan, one of the security guards from the lab, and the blonde graduate student. I didn't recognize any of the others.

A sound in the hall sent a chill through me. Closing the drawer I had open, I hurried into a corner and blended into the background just as a man in scrubs and a long lab coat came in the room. I knew Ron had people working for him, but I'd failed to consider that when I made my reconnaissance. I stood still as I watched the worker go about his business.

He opened a drawer less than six feet from me and pulled the body out of it. It appeared to be a woman, and from her injuries, I guessed she died from some kind of accident. Half her head was caved in, and she had cuts and bruises to her face. He wheeled her to the door, then out. The last I could see, he took her across the hall.

I breathed a sigh of relief and surveyed the room. That was the only door. I started toward it, but a soft bumping sound preceded the door opening again. I leaped against a wall and froze. The guy came back and pulled another body out of its drawer, then took it across the hall. I decided I'd wait a little longer before I moved again.

After five minutes, I decided he wasn't coming back, so I slipped out the door and down the hall. The halls didn't have any recesses or alcoves I could hide in. Blending in was fine, but not if someone bumped into me. It also would be kind of noticeable if someone looked down a long hallway and saw a human-shaped lump on the wall.

I made it to the showroom, and decided it would be safer to go out the front door rather than try and make it back the way I'd come. I was halfway around the room when I heard two men talking and coming toward me. I ducked into an empty office and dived under the desk. The next thing I knew, the office door closed.

"That was the bloody stupidest thing I've ever seen in my life." The voice was Gareth Blaine's. "Why did you go after Bouchard?"

"He went to Alonzo. How the hell was I supposed to know the old man lives in a fortress?" Jimmy

Alderette's voice. "And you're a fine one to talk about stupid. If it wasn't for you, we wouldn't have lost the Dallas operation. Why did you try to hit the Nelson broad?"

"I thought I could take her out and get Simon Wellington off my back," Blaine said.

One of them walked around the desk, pulled out the chair, and dropped into it. His foot came within an inch of my hand.

"Then there's this mess," Alderette said. "Billy's asking questions about what happened to his father, and my wife isn't real happy about it either."

Blaine walked around a bit. The office wasn't large enough to walk much. It definitely wasn't big enough for that conversation with me hiding under the desk. I was scrunched up so much I couldn't reach a weapon. If they found me, I'd have to draw as I sprang out at them, assuming my legs hadn't fallen asleep.

"Tell Billy that Liz Nelson killed his father," Blaine said. "Give him her address, and also the address of that bloody orphanage she funds. And for God's sake, give him some direction. Don't just turn him loose and hope he does what you want him to. Tell him to follow her and take her out at the orphanage, not at her house. I'm willing to bet an attack on her house would be as much of a failure as that fiasco last night."

"That might work," Alderette said.

"I wouldn't bet on it, but if it doesn't, we'll be quit of Billy bloody Smythe.

"We'll still have Wilberforce to deal with."

"Wilberforce will be easy to take care of once the Nelson bitch is gone. She does all his thinking for him."

"Have you found the Sheridan woman yet?"

180

Alderette asked.

"No, and Campbell swears he doesn't know where she is."

"I still think he's protecting her."

"I don't think so," Blaine said. "He knows she's a weak link, especially after her brother died. Campbell's strong. I'm not worried about him. You point Billy in the right direction and hope he takes care of our major problem."

It took me some time to uncurl from under the desk after they left. Checking my chrono, I realized the service was over. I had no idea who might be wandering around, or what would be the best way to get out of there.

No one was in the showroom, so I raced across the room and unlocked the door. I had it half open when I heard someone coming down the hall from where all the bodies were. Letting loose of the door handle, I whirled around and faced the room. Ron walked in and pulled up short, looking at me in surprise.

"May I help you?"

I was still wearing the old lady illusion. "I was at the service," I said, "and I wondered about the prices of the caskets. I'm not getting any younger, you know. Poor Fred was even younger than I am."

I endured Ron's sales pitch, including him trying to sell me casket, plot, and funeral in advance. I didn't know you could pay for a funeral on a ten-year loan. The interest rate was exorbitant, though.

I finally escaped, taking the route by the neighbors with all the trees. Retrieving my

181

motorcycle, I headed home, checking constantly to see if anyone was following me.

⊕⊕⊕

CHAPTER 16

I came home to find Dad set up on my back porch, ready to grill a couple of steaks. When I left that morning, I didn't have steaks or corn in the fridge, let alone a grill. Of course, at his house the back porch was enclosed with an exhaust setup for the grill.

"You have my permission to kill Gareth Blaine," Dad said when he heard my news.

"Just as soon as Wil transfers my contract to his budget, I will. I want to make sure I get paid for performing that kind of public service."

He plopped a medium-rare steak on my plate along with corn on the cob and potato salad.

"Where did all this come from?"

"Don't speak with your mouth full. I had it delivered. A couple of Noah's boys brought the grill from my place."

"You can have groceries delivered? Does the liquor store do that?"

He laughed. "Yes, and yes. I hate grocery stores. The aisles are too narrow for my chair. Liquor stores are worse."

We paid strict attention to our food for a while, but when we finished and he poured cordials and coffee, he said, "So what now?"

"I need to go warn Amanda Rollins and see what I can do to arrange some sort of security for the place. Maybe I can talk Wil into a raid on that drug house where Billy Smythe does his business."

"Remember, gangbangers are crazy, and often not too bright. They don't act and react like a rational opponent." Dad fell into lecture mode at the drop of a hat. I'd never understood why Mom found that sexy,

183

but she spent a whole semester listening to him before she banged him and ended up with me.

"Yeah, I know. It always boggles me that they see people killed all the time, but don't think it will happen to them. There's some kind of disconnect in their brains. I don't know if it's the drugs, breathing unfiltered air, congenital issues, or what. With a lot of them, it seems as though their danger reaction is broken."

"How's your danger reaction?" he asked.

I pulled down the neck of my shirt so he could see the corset. "In the words of my illustrious sire, more people are killed by accident than intentionally. I've never seen a gangbanger who could shoot worth a damn. I could get hit by a bullet aimed at someone else."

I did the dishes, then headed out. The guards Talbot had put on my place were discretely but obviously present, which made me feel better. I didn't know if the place was being watched or not, but I morphed into a likeness of Noah Talbot when I left the house.

First stop was The Pinnacle. I dropped a word with Paul about Billy Smythe and showed the bouncers his picture. Then I sat down with Nellie.

"This guy," I said, showing her Smythe's picture, "is gunning for me. I got a tip that he might try to target me at Miz Rollins' place."

She didn't say a word, just stood up and walked over to where her brother Tom was working the door. They spoke for a few minutes, with an occasional glance toward me.

Nellie came back, sat down, and took a swallow from her drink. "Tom said he'll make a few calls. You piss someone off, that's your business and I'll let you handle it. Aunt Amanda is family. Nobody messes with family in my neighborhood."

I held up my glass and she clinked hers against it.

That taken care of, I called Wil.

"Libby? To what do I owe this honor?"

"I'd like to buy you a drink."

"Business or pleasure?"

"I like to think that any time spent in my presence is pleasurable."

I heard him laughing. "I'm sure you do. Okay, give me half an hour. Where should I meet you?"

I told Tom that I'd be upstairs and climbed the stairs to find a table in one of the out-of-the-way corners. One of the things I'd noticed about Wil was he was punctual. He climbed the stairs twenty-nine minutes after I hung up the phone.

"What happened to you?" he said as he sat down. "I had three people at the funeral, two inside and one watching outside, and you never showed."

"I was there. I guess your people aren't very observant."

He squinted at me. "So, you missed me?"

"I did." The waitress came and took his order. "Wil, you have something I just can't live without."

He clapped his hand on his wallet and I laughed.

"Very perceptive. I need you to pick up my contract with the Chamber."

"And why would I do that?"

"So that I can continue working on this case after I kill Gareth Blaine. I also need you to organize a raid on that drug house."

"Oookaaay. What happened?"

"Blaine and Alderette set Billy Smythe on me.

185

Gave him my address and suggested he ambush me at the orphanage I support."

I took a drink and stared out at the dance floor below while I debated if I should tell him the rest.

"I also found out that he put a hit out on me earlier, when Simon Wellington first suggested hiring me."

Wil was quiet for some time, then he said, "And how did you learn all of this?"

"I heard Blaine and Alderette talking at the mortuary."

"Overheard their conversation. I see. And where were you?"

"Hiding under the desk in the office they chose to accuse each other of incompetence."

Another short period of silence, then he snorted and cracked up. "You...are the...most unbelievable person...I ever met," he managed between bouts of laughter.

"I'm glad that people threatening my life are such a source of amusement for you." I didn't see anything funny about the situation.

He wound down, wiping tears from his eyes. "I'm not even going to ask how you ended up under a desk."

"That mortuary is where Alderette sends his dead," I said. "I assume Blaine uses it, too. Those guys from the airport, Sheridan and one of his lab assistants, and one of the security guards were all there. I'll bet some bodies that no one knows about end up there, too."

"Isn't that your boyfriend's business?" Wil asked.

"Yeah. So?"

"So, doesn't that implicate him?"

"No. Why would it? He's a businessman. If I were in the body business, I'd want the contract with the two largest criminal organizations in town."

"And those are?"

"The Chamber of Commerce and the Donofrio family, of course."

"Of course. And the Bouchard-Nelson family is third?"

"I resent that. My father was defending himself. Are you going to pick up my contract, or not?"

He acted as though he was thinking. I knew he was trying to figure out how to squeeze me to his benefit.

"Why don't you come to work for me full time?"

Oh, no. Most corporations had strict policies on employees sleeping with their bosses, and I wasn't ready to give up my Wilbur fantasies. That wasn't the main reason though. I shook my head.

"I couldn't afford the pay cut."

"You haven't heard my offer."

"The answer is no. I'll take a retainer to be on call, but we'll negotiate contracts on a case-by-case basis. Don't change the subject."

Wil forcefully blew out his breath and nodded. He pulled out his phone, made a call, and told the person on the other end to transfer my contract from the local Toronto office to the continental office.

"Happy?" he asked as he tucked his phone away.

"Ecstatic. Now I can blow that bastard's brains out."

He chuckled. "You seem like such a nice girl until one gets to know you. You didn't happen to find Diane Sheridan, did you?"

"No, but I looked. If she's dead, they disposed of her body somewhere else."

⊕⊕⊕

I met with Wil and a couple of his men at a hotel the following day. We viewed recordings from the Chamber's drones for almost two hours, studied maps, and made plans for an assault. They told me it would take them another day to airlift in a SWAT team.

That was all right with me. I went home and tried to make myself presentable for my date with Ron. I had forgotten what it was like to go out on a date with my father around.

"You're still going on a date?" he asked.

"Yes, why?"

"Earth to Libby. Someone is trying to kill you."

"So, what am I supposed to do? Hide under my bed and hope they forget about me? Johnny Jack is only going to be here one night, and at his age, this might be my last chance to see him."

Dad shook his head and frowned.

"I'll be careful. I promise."

"At least you could wear shoes you can run in if you have to."

I looked down at my heels. He was probably right, and Ron wasn't that tall. I changed them for a pair of calf-high boots with two-inch heels.

"Happy?" I asked him.

"Those are better, I guess. Are you going to be home tonight? I'm only asking so I know how long to wait before I send people out looking for your body."

"Dad, leave it alone. I'll call you, okay?"

I still had an hour before I met Ron, so I jumped on the computer. A couple of searches turned up empty. In spite of all the witnesses, I couldn't find any mention of two young men dropping dead at the airport.

Even more surprising, a small war in an upscale residential neighborhood wasn't worth reporting. No mention of my dad's house being bombed or men machine-gunned in his front yard. There must have been a hundred corporate agents, cops, EMTs, and assorted other personnel there all night. Totally invisible.

When I mentioned it to Dad, he simply shrugged. "The media is corporate owned."

"But how do we know what's true? How do you find out what's really happening?"

He gave me the kind of look you give a puppy that trips over its own feet.

⊕⊕⊕

Ron and I met at a popular café near The Crown Royal. When we sat down, I turned the tables on him.

"How's business?" I asked.

His head jerked up. "Uh, it's okay."

"I was wondering. There's been a lot on the newscasts about drug overdoses. A family I did some work for lost their son that way."

He seemed to be a little lost, fishing for an answer.

"I was out at the airport the other day to meet a friend who flew in, and saw two men collapse and die, right there in the terminal. I wondered if they were on drugs."

I ordered through the automenu and looked to him. He hastily paged through the menu and submitted his order. Our beers slid out of the delivery chute and I took a drink of mine.

"You haven't seen any of that?" I asked.

"A little bit. Not too much."

"Hmph. It figures. The media probably made a big deal of a couple of rich kids getting snuffed."

"Yeah, maybe," he said.

The concert was great. Johnny Jack was in fine form, telling funny stories between songs and interacting with the audience. The music was everything I hoped for—strong, driving, Mississippi Delta blues. Of course, at the time the genre was created, the Mississippi Delta was two hundred miles farther south than when he was born.

Afterward, we strolled down the street and stopped in at a tavern for a drink. I hadn't been in the place since my university days, but it hadn't changed much. Except for the luvdaze. It was as bad as the Drop Inn. We found a small booth, and I had to brush three jet injectors off the seat before I sat down.

"This is what I was talking about," I said. His brow furrowed as he tried to put my statement into some kind of context. "The drugs."

"Oh." His face cleared. "Yeah, it's a little up front, isn't it?"

A couple of booths down, a guy and a girl were trying to rouse another girl. From her complexion and the way her head was rolling around loosely, I feared the worse. Getting up, I walked over and leaned close, placing my fingers on her temple to feel for a pulse.

She wasn't breathing. She couldn't have been older than eighteen or nineteen, and tiny, barely five feet tall. A dosage meant for a grown man would be too much for her, but of course, drug dealers didn't think that way.

I went to the bar and grabbed a bartender by the arm.

"Hey," he said, "wait your turn. I'll get to you." He was young, probably a student working part time.

Yanking him toward me, I snarled in his face. "You see that girl over there in the booth? She's dead. I suggest you call an ambulance. Now."

He turned pasty white and reached for a phone.

Ron watched me from our booth. I walked back to him and said, "Let's get out of here."

As we walked to the door, he asked, "Is she dead?"

"Yeah. I saw it happen a couple of weeks ago. I guess this new drug doesn't have much room for error."

We went back to Ron's. I knew that Ron worked with dead people all the time, but so did I. It kind of bothered me that the girl's OD didn't seem to bother him at all.

He opened the front door of his house, and I stepped through into the foyer. The door to my right was open, and several caskets were stacked on rack-like pallets, as though they were being moved. Peering closer, I saw shipping labels on them.

"Business must be good," I commented. "Are those new, or are there bodies in them?"

"A group of tourists were killed in an accident," he said. "We're shipping the bodies back to their homes."

I stepped closer and read the labels. Montreal, Chicago, Buffalo, and Calgary. "They certainly were an eclectic bunch," I said. "No two of them from the same town?"

"University students. The bodies are going to their parents." He pulled the door closed and took me in his arms. "I'd rather think about someone warm and living, such as you." He kissed me.

⊕⊕⊕

I called Gareth Blaine the next morning and asked for a meeting. He set it for an upscale restaurant at lunchtime.

The arms vault in my spare bedroom contained a small refrigerator. I sprayed my hands and forearms with a sealer, put on surgical gloves and my filter mask, then took a tiny vial from the fridge. Putting a drop from the vial on a small piece of special paper and sealing the paper in a plastic bag completed my preparations for the meeting.

Forensics teams used the spray sealer to prevent contaminating a crime scene, but it also prevented my skin absorbing foreign substances and sealed my fingerprints.

Blaine and I walked into the restaurant at almost the same time and the host conducted us to a table off to the side. I saw that the spacing between tables was larger than most restaurants, ensuring more privacy. All of the patrons except me were wearing suits.

He looked a little nervous. "What is this about?" he asked after the waiter brought us drinks.

I glanced around, licking my lips. "I think we have a problem. How well do you know Wilbur Wilberforce?"

His eyes narrowed, he seemed to relax slightly,

and he leaned forward. "I know him professionally. Other than that, not very well. Why?"

"I think we have a leak inside the investigation. I think there's a corporate connection to the drug, and that someone is tipping them off."

"That's a very serious allegation."

"I'm not accusing him. I don't know where the leak is coming from, but he's the outsider here. You and I are from Toronto and have local connections."

"When you say a corporate connection to the drug, what do you mean?"

I glanced around again and dropped my voice even lower. "I think CanPharm is producing the drug either in a secret lab, or maybe in one of their production facilities after hours. Then they're shipping it with legitimate products to other cities." I was lying through my teeth, but thought I should give him something plausible and near the truth.

"And how are they distributing it?"

"Here in Toronto, through the Donofrio crime family. I assume they're using similar channels in other places."

I whipped my head to the side, eyes wide, as though I'd seen something startling. Blaine turned his head to look and I dropped my little piece of paper in his drink. The paper dissolved immediately.

"What?" he asked, turning back to me.

"Nothing. I thought I saw one of Alonzo Donofrio's men come in, but I was mistaken. Mr. Blaine, I want out of this. The mob has already attacked my father. I'm scared." I took a swallow of my drink.

"Let me check into a few things," he said. "Maybe you should just lie low for a while."

193

"I think that's a good idea. Thank you."

I picked up my drink and drained it. "Thank you for meeting with me."

He took a swallow of his drink and said, "Not a problem, Miss Nelson. And thank you for the information concerning a leak. I will certainly look into it."

I stood to go. Blaine pushed his card into the payment slot on the table, drank the rest of his drink, and stood. We walked out together, going our separate ways at the sidewalk.

Botulinum toxin was the most lethal poison known. I'd put enough in Blaine's drink to kill the legendary elephant. It would be a shocker if he survived the night.

I stepped into an alley halfway down the block and blended into the wall. A couple of minutes later, a man stuck his head around the corner. Not seeing me, he rushed into the alley with a second man trailing him. Both of them carried pistols.

They ran to the end of the alley and onto the next street. I waited half an hour, then took a circuitous route back to where I'd left my motorcycle.

CHAPTER 17

The following afternoon, I met Wil and his SWAT team inside a Chamber-owned training facility near the airport. One wall had a screen showing the drug house as viewed by the camera of a drone that had landed on a rooftop across the street. Other than a couple of gang members loitering around the entrance, the place looked deserted.

When I walked in, Wil raised an eyebrow and ushered me into an office off to the side of the conference room.

"Gareth Blaine died this morning," he said.

"Unpleasantly, I hope."

"So it would seem. He was alone, but the ME thinks it was some kind of food poisoning."

"He probably swallowed one of his own lies." I met Wil's eyes. "Couldn't have happened to a nicer guy. You know he sent a couple of hitmen after me yesterday, don't you?"

"No, I wasn't aware of that. How do you know it was Gareth?"

"One of them was the guy with the port wine birthmark near his left eye." I pointed to the outer office where I had walked past that very guy only a couple of minutes before.

Wil's eyes widened. "You mean the guy out there?"

"Yes. I didn't see his buddy this morning. Dark hair and skin, big nose, has a tattoo of a spider on his left hand."

He got wild-eyed and rushed out of the room, stopping to confer with someone I didn't recognize, who then got on his radio. A few minutes later, I heard a short commotion in the outer room, and Mr. Port Wine was brought in by half a dozen armed SWAT officers.

"Were you ordered to hit someone yesterday?" Wil asked him.

"I don't report to you," the man said, "and I'm not at liberty to discuss confidential business."

"I'll take that as a yes," Wil said. He turned to another man wearing a suit. "I'm going to have to assume that anyone who isn't cooperative is involved in Blaine's conspiracy."

Turning back to the SWAT troops, he said, "Lock him up. When you find Karim, lock him up, too, but not together."

"Wait! I was just following orders, but we didn't kill anyone. The girl disappeared."

"But you would have killed me if you caught me?" I stormed forward and everyone took a step back. Port Wine didn't back up far enough. I have very long legs, and my foot between his legs almost lifted him off the ground.

Maybe it wasn't very mature of me, but it was awfully satisfying watching him curled up on the floor, vomiting on himself. The rest of the men in the room looked a little paler than they did earlier.

"Get him out of here," Wil ordered, and the SWAT team dragged my assailant out.

Wil turned to me, but before he could say anything, I said, "I guess I should have killed them yesterday, but I thought you'd be happy I showed some restraint."

Wil shut his mouth. I batted my eyes at him and smiled.

"Miss Elizabeth Nelson," he said, turning to the man in the suit, "this is Alexi Morales, the new head of security for the Chamber's Toronto office."

"Pleased to make your acquaintance, Miss Nelson," he said. I noticed he didn't come close enough to shake hands. "I hope we have a better working relationship than you had with my predecessor."

I wondered how it could be worse.

"You wouldn't happen to know anything about Gareth's demise, would you?" Morales asked. "I understand you had lunch with him yesterday."

"No, I met him for a drink, but neither of us ate anything. Maybe he got something from a food cart." The itinerant food carts were notorious for a list of food-borne diseases. A lot of chili kills some bacteria and fungi, but not others, and it doesn't do a thing for viruses.

Neither Morales nor Wil seemed to appreciate my suggestion.

We sat around and planned for the next two hours, or that's what they called it. What they were really doing was waiting for dark. I didn't understand why they wanted the gangbangers to be awake. I would've hit them at noon, when they were asleep. I had that itchy feeling that made me want to move, to go someplace. I tried to figure out exactly what the feeling was, or what it meant. I decided I was just tired of waiting, but it didn't make it any easier to sit still.

"You know, in that neighborhood, it might be better to attack them before dark," I said at one point, only to receive a lecture about night-vision goggles and the element of surprise and a few other things that I didn't pay much attention to.

"Yeah, but they'll be awake after dark. They're mostly sleeping right now. Everyone in that neighborhood is probably asleep."

Morales gave me one of those girls-should-stay-in-the-kitchen-and-bedroom kind of paternalistic smiles.

Finally, the SWAT team got it together, and we prepared to board the three helicopters awaiting us. Wil held out a flak jacket.

"I don't need that, but thanks."

"Oh, you're bullet proof now?"

"No." I pulled up my t-shirt and showed him my corset. "Kevlar and ballistic cloth."

To my surprise, he blushed. I was tempted to take his hand and ask him if my bra felt familiar, but I restrained myself.

We swooped in on the drug house, just like in a vid. One of the helicopters hovered over the building, one sat down on the roof of an adjacent building, and the third, the one Wil and I rode in, landed in the only clear space on the ground about thirty yards from the entrance.

The SWAT team fanned out toward the building from our copter while the team on the other building's roof descended the stairs there. No sooner did both teams enter the buildings than they ran into resistance.

I crouched outside behind an old junk car and listened to all the shooting and screaming. I thought with all their drone surveillance, they should have noticed the drug house wasn't the only inhabited building in the area. Maybe they didn't pay attention to what went on after dark.

A sound behind me caused me to turn, and I saw a

girl and boy rushing up behind me. I fired at him, hitting him in the chest, but she slammed into me before I could get another shot off. She bore me to the ground, and I hit the back of my head. Stars and comets. Her weight on top of me and her knee in my stomach made it hard to fight back.

I managed to get my arm up between us and hold her mouth away from my throat. She was strong, and it took me a few moments to regain my senses, then I began hitting her in the head with the pistol I still held in my other hand.

A shadow loomed above us. The boy I'd shot leaned down to grab my arm. I reacted just in time, shooting him in the face.

My distraction allowed his girlfriend to push off from me and grab my free arm. She pulled my wrist to her open mouth at the same time as I pushed the muzzle of my gun against her temple and pulled the trigger.

Rolling her off me, I saw Wil running toward me.

"Are you all right?" he asked, his head turning back and forth from me to the two kids I'd shot. Neither of them could have been eighteen yet.

"Yeah, I think so." I looked beyond him, took aim, and fired. With a little more time, my bullet took the boy in the head and he went down.

"What the hell is going on?" he asked. "Who are these people?" His face betrayed confusion.

"You don't know?"

"Know what?"

"Oh, hell. Why do you think I wanted to hit this place in the daytime? This is a vampire neighborhood. At least half of the gang members I saw on your video going in and out of that house are vamps."

"Vampires? Why didn't you tell us?"

I shot another one who was sneaking up on us. "I tried. Couldn't you see? Don't any of you know what a vamp looks like? Why did you think their skin was so white?" I couldn't believe it. I was dealing with corporate idiots. "All you had to do was look at one of the police maps. Here be vampires. Go about six blocks in that direction," I pointed, "and you'll be up to your ass in lycanthropes. The bar around the next corner is called Fang, and the nightclub two blocks away is called Bloodlust."

Wil stared at me gape mouthed.

I shook my head. "How long have you lived in Toronto? East of the sewage treatment plant is the mutie district. You could have asked any ten year old on the street."

For the most part, vamps left people alone. They fed on us, of course, but I probably could have walked through the neighborhood at night without them hassling me. But they answered an assault on their territory the same way any other group would defend their homes.

Too damned late to fix it. "Let's get out of the street," I said, grabbing him by the arm. "If you don't want to go in the house, then we can help defend that chopper on the ground."

We reached the helicopter on the ground and jumped in the back, turning to face outwards. A terrible screeching sound came from above us. We looked up and saw dozens of people pushing the other helicopter on the roof. The chopper was firing its machineguns, but many of those attacking it were under the level of the guns, or to the side.

As we watched, the mob pushed the machine to the edge of the roof, and then over. It hit the street with a tremendous crash.

"God help your SWAT team that entered that building," I said. Hundreds of vamps swarmed the area.

Wil clambered up to the cockpit and talked with the pilots, then got on the radio. The copter still hovering over the scene dropped a half-dozen gas canisters. I pulled a different mask out of my bag and slapped it on. Some security systems utilized gas, so I always had a gas mask handy. Losing consciousness in a place you were robbing was usually very embarrassing.

The helicopter in the air moved over the tenement where the other copter had landed and dropped more gas. A few minutes later, more helicopters arrived.

⊕⊕⊕

Morning light revealed a hellish scene. Several buildings that had stood the previous day were reduced to rubble. Bodies lay everywhere. Most were knocked out from the gas, but too many were dead, including half the Chamber's SWAT team. Most of the vamps were young. The vampire mutation didn't usually lead to a long life. Unless they were rich, there was rarely any penalty for killing them, and exile to the slums was dangerous for anyone—normal, mutie, vampire, or rat.

We confiscated a huge stash of drugs. Heroin, luvdaze, cocaine, amphetamines, barbiturates and many more. Credit cards linked to accounts with millions of credits. Billy and his gang were big time.

What we didn't find was Billy. We did find a couple of computers. Wil sent them to his forensics people, hoping to find records that would lead us to the luvdaze lab. I didn't plan to hold my breath.

Wil dropped me off at my house. Dad was awake, and after assuring himself that I was unharmed, sent me to take a shower while he fixed me breakfast.

Standing in the shower under the stream of hot water, I discovered various scrapes and bruises, including a thin gash on my wrist from one of the girl's fangs. The lump on the back of my head was the size of an egg and hurt like hell.

"I couldn't believe it," I told Dad for about the tenth time as I ate my breakfast. "The bloody idiots didn't know we were dropping into the heaviest concentration of vamps in Ontario."

"The corporations don't look down," Dad said. "They employ local police to deal with street crime. They don't pay much attention to muties unless one of their own kids is mutated." He poured me some more orange juice. "What are you going to do now?"

"Go to bed and sleep for a week."

"Best plan I've heard lately."

My phone rang. I couldn't think of anyone I wanted to talk to, so I checked who was calling before I answered it. Amanda Rollins.

"Hello? Miz Rollins?"

"Libby, there's a couple of gangbangers here lookin for you. One has a white Mohawk, and the other's a vamp."

"Lock all your doors," I said as I bolted for the bedroom. "I'll be there as soon as I can. Call Tom."

I threw on some clothes, grabbed my bag, and jumped on my motorcycle. I broke enough laws getting there—speeding, weaving in and out of traffic, running traffic lights, driving across a park—to get my

202

permit revoked. The thought of Billy and a vamp hurting Amanda or the kids made me sick. I swore he'd die slowly.

Arriving at the school, I surveyed the area and didn't see anything that looked out of place. Some of the kids were playing in the yard. Billy Smythe and another man were sitting on the front steps. I jumped off the motorcycle and ran up to them, a knife in one hand and my pistol in the other.

Billy looked up at me with an idiot smile on his face. I couldn't see any spark of intelligence in his eyes, and he was drooling on himself. His friend, the vamp, was in the same shape. Amanda leaned against the doorframe with her arms crossed.

Hello, Miz Libby, Walter's voice sounded in my head. *They wanted to hurt Miz Rollins and they planned to hurt you. I couldn't let that happen.*

I looked around, and didn't see him. "Miz Rollins?" I called to her.

"You didn't wait for me to explain when I called," she said. "I was goin to tell ya that we had things under control. But these two can't stay here. Do ya have someone to take em?"

"Are...are they going to stay like this?" I asked.

They won't hurt anyone ever again, Walter told me. *They weren't nice people.*

I wasn't sure what to do. I couldn't leave them on Amanda's doorstep. Checking their pockets, I discovered they both had legitimate identification.

A shadow fell over me, and I glanced up to find Amanda standing there.

"Walter is very protective," she said.

"I think that's great, but I don't know what to do with them."

203

"Take them to the subway or light rail, put them on a train, and leave them when you get off at the next stop. There's a charity that will take them."

"You're kidding." I gazed into her eyes and saw only sorrow and kindness.

"Really."

So that's what I did. They didn't even notice when I got off the train and left them.

CHAPTER 18

I was back to square one as far as my original goal, which was to get the luvdaze drug off the streets. All of my leads back to the drug's origin were either dead or mind dead.

Diane Sheridan's bank accounts still showed zero activity. She was either dead or using a pseudonym that I could not identify. Liam Campbell was the only principal in the original scheme still left. I ran some queries and set myself to follow him.

The next morning, my takeout mocha and I sat across the street from Campbell's luxury apartment building. I sat there a long time. Campbell evidently was a late riser and didn't emerge until nine o'clock. He got in a limo that, to my dismay, rose into the air and flew off. Little chance of me following him on my motorcycle.

At eight o'clock that evening, he walked out of the CanPharm office building where he worked, got in the limo, and flew off again. Aircars were a decided luxury, and one I didn't have any access to. Hell, the only person I knew who had access to an aircar was Nellie's sugar daddy.

I rode by Campbell's apartment and saw lights in the windows, but had no idea whether he was there or not. Frustrated, I went home, hacked into his computer accounts, and accessed his schedule. I noticed recurring private appointments on Friday evenings. Deeper investigation suggested they were with a woman. Cross checking with Diane Sheridan's calendar cleared up the issue. I checked out the dates in the future and in the past. The future ones were just placeholders. Evidently, he filled in the details as he needed to, if he needed to. None of the appointments after her brother's death contained any details.

On the whole, Campbell's schedule was problematic. He didn't seem to keep it up to date. With few exceptions, it only recorded working meetings, and except for the appointment with Diane, he didn't schedule anything outside of normal work hours.

The next day, after the limo picked up Campbell in the morning, I sat back and waited. About two hours later, his wife Cynthia came out and got in a taxi. As soon as it drove off, I morphed into his likeness and crossed the street. I had accessed his apartment building's security system and programmed my own passcode that morning. It took a little longer to get into his apartment, but fifteen minutes after Cynthia locked the door, I stood in their living room. Nice place.

I spent two hours searching the apartment and found nothing that could tie Campbell to any of the people I knew were involved with the drug ring. I didn't find anything to indicate Diane Sheridan had ever been there. Of course, I didn't know how much his wife knew about Diane. I wondered how Diane felt about him continuing to live with his ex. Seemed pretty weird to me.

I resigned myself to a long surveillance. Sooner or later, he'd break with the routine. I planted half a dozen bugs throughout the apartment, then called Wil and arranged to meet with him for lunch.

Nellie called as I waited for Wil.

"Hey, girlfriend. Long time, no see. Can you talk?"

"Sure, Nellie. I have an appointment in a few minutes, though."

"I'll keep it short. Don't forget that the charity concert for the orphanage is this Saturday. Be there by noon at the latest. Okay?"

"Damn. I forgot."

"That's why I called to remind you. We got two more local bands to play intro. The music starts at three o'clock. Food vendors, some corporate sponsors. Artists gonna sell their work with ten percent to the orphanage. We sold two thousand tickets already. We gonna rock the hood, baby." I could hear the smile in her voice.

"I'll be there." For one day, I could have a good time and forget all the crap surrounding luvdaze.

When Wil showed up, I filled him in on what I had learned.

"I'm going to need help tailing Campbell. Do you think we can ask for help from that Mateo Hudiburg guy?"

He shook his head. "Campbell is too high up. His position is at the VP level. We don't have any proof. We don't have any witnesses or evidence tying him to the drug."

"But CanPharm employees are dead," I said. "A CanPharm lab was broken into and pillaged. Surely Hudiburg can investigate that."

"University employees, university lab. CanPharm is out its grant money, but that's Campbell's problem. When you're funding research, you expect to spend a lot of money on dead ends. The one that hits and makes billions covers it all."

"So, you're saying we just drop it?"

"I'm not saying that at all. Simon Wellington wants the drug off the street, and Hudson Bay is one of the largest corporations on the continent. He doesn't pay the Chamber to ignore his concerns. I'm just saying that unless we have proof, Campbell is off limits. We can investigate him discretely, but we can't accuse him."

Wil appeared as frustrated as I felt.

"What about the other cities?" I asked. "Any idea who is distributing the drug there? How they're getting it? I mean, we know who was doing it in Dallas. With Blaine gone, who are they getting it from now?"

He stared off into space and I could almost hear his mind churning. When he turned back to me, he said, "Except for Dallas and Ottawa, all the distribution seems to be through mob channels."

"Alderette."

"Yes."

⊕⊕⊕

That afternoon I managed to sneak up on Campbell's limo and plant a bug and a tracer on it while the driver waited for him.

Wil set a couple of drones to follow Campbell's limo and told the drone operators to alert me if he went anywhere unusual.

Out of curiosity, I decided to follow his wife the next day. The couple lived well, but within the exorbitant salary CanPharm paid him. In spite of the enormous sums he was depositing in his accounts, he hadn't bought a yacht or anything. He put an allowance in his ex-wife's account every month, and that amount hadn't changed much over the past couple of years.

Cynthia Campbell did have some rather unusual expenses that puzzled me. A couple of times a week she paid individuals a couple of hundred credits.

Occasionally the same name came up more than once, but in general, these were one-time payments. I checked on two or three of the people, and found they were far from the social class with which I would expect her to socialize.

On those days, she also made payments to a ritzy little bistro in the entertainment district and to another business identified by its bank account as Front Door Enterprises.

Following Cynthia was boring. She spent the morning shopping but not buying very much. Then she went to the bistro for lunch, and I discovered she was meeting Alice Alderette and Sophia Gonzales, Alonzo Donofrio's daughter. An interesting trio. All had husbands connected to the illegal drug trade.

While they ate and chatted, I pulled out my tablet and a stylus and started trying to chart out the connections between the players in that scheme. I was totally confused as to who all the players were and how they fit together. A few online queries helped fill in the blanks. When I finished, I sat back and tried to take it all in.

It was a face-palm moment. No wonder Ron's business, Calderone Funeral Home, did business with Jimmy Alderette. Sophia's former husband was Ron's cousin.

What I had was a family affair. The only one I hadn't identified until then was Ron, who was a cousin to Cynthia as well as to Sophia's ex-husband. The question was whether Ron had a part in the scheme or simply benefited from all the dead bodies.

I thought of the caskets I'd seen that night at Ron's, the ones labeled for shipment to other cities. Cities with a luvdaze problem.

The women finished their lunch and said their

goodbyes on the sidewalk. I followed Cynthia Campbell.

She strolled down the street, doing a bit of window shopping, and soon crossed into a less savory neighborhood. That surprised me a bit, and I wondered what she was searching for. A couple more blocks, a twist and a turn, and she was walking down a street where boys and girls, some as young as ten or twelve, others as old as I was, displayed themselves for sale.

Halfway down the street, she stopped, then crooked her finger. A lad I judged to be about twenty pushed away from the wall. They exchanged a few words, then she turned and walked on with him following her. When they reached the corner, she turned into the doorway of a hotel that rented rooms by the hour.

Having absolutely no interest in knowing what she did in there, I kept going.

⊕⊕⊕

"I think I know how they're shipping the drugs to other cities," I told Wil when I met him that evening. "I still have to confirm it. But I'm going to watch the shipping point and see if I can spot a delivery."

He motioned toward my ear. "Are you still wearing the tracker I gave you?"

I grinned and bit down on the little device squeezed between my last tooth and cheek. "Can you hear me now?"

"Perfectly," he said, returning my grin. I loved his smile and the light dancing in his eyes.

"You know," Wil continued, "I thought you'd be

difficult to work with. Consultants often are. But I've been pleasantly surprised by how cooperative you've been."

The light was hitting the planes of his face in a manner that made him seem like the subject of a painting. That led to thoughts of how lovely a nude painting of him would look in my bedroom. I wasn't sure I wanted the real thing in my bedroom, but a painting would be nice.

I realized he'd stopped talking and seemed to be expecting some sort of response.

"I'm sorry, Wil, I was spacing out."

"I asked if you were hungry. Would you like to catch some dinner?"

Thinking back over my day, I realized I hadn't eaten since breakfast. "You have some of the most marvelous ideas. Where shall we go?"

His first idea was tempting, but wouldn't fly unless we went home to change. Reservations made a week earlier also would have helped. I made an alternative suggestion, and that was where we ended up.

On the way to our table, I spotted a couple of familiar faces, and I made sure to sit where I could see them. I hadn't known Sophia Gonzales was dating again, but I didn't make a point of following her life. She was two years a widow, so I shouldn't have been surprised. Whom she was eating with was a surprise, however. Her deceased husband's cousin, Ron Calderone.

Brian Gonzales had chafed under Alonzo's control and what Alonzo thought was appropriate for his daughter's husband. Brian started freelancing, getting into the drug business, which was one business Alonzo despised. Alonzo warned him, but Brian continued. His defiance was something Alonzo couldn't tolerate. He paid me half a million to make it look like an accident and take his secret to my grave.

Seeing Sophia with Cynthia and Alice earlier, and now with Ron, stretched my acceptance of coincidence.

"You've been distracted all night," Wil said. "What's going on?"

"New information. We knew some personal relationships were involved in this thing, but the family connections are even deeper than we suspected." I showed him the chart I'd made that afternoon.

"You think the wives are involved?" Wil sounded skeptical.

"I think we've had Alderette and Campbell under surveillance and we aren't getting any closer to figuring out the puzzle. I'm sure that Blaine warned them. If they aren't taking a personal hand in things, who do you think they trust?"

I rode my motorcycle over to Ron's place early the next morning. All the trees on the property next to the funeral home made a great place for a chameleon to settle in and watch Ron's operation. Around sundown on the second day of my vigil, a car pulled up to the back of the funeral home and Alice Alderette got out. Before she reached the back door, it opened and Ron came out to greet her.

He carried several boxes from her car into the building, then Alice got back in her car and drove away.

I wanted to go inside to check and see if my supposed boyfriend was loading drugs into caskets to ship all over the continent. His security was fairly basic, so getting in wouldn't be a problem. What would anyone want to steal from a funeral home?

The lights in the business side went out about an hour later. I figured it was only a matter of time before Ron went out, as he did almost every night. I waited until midnight when the light turned off in his bedroom. It was just my luck that the one night he stayed in was the night I wanted him to go tom catting.

I went home, planning to go back to the funeral home the following night. Hopefully, he wouldn't ship the drugs immediately.

Nellie called while I was eating breakfast. "Is your dad coming today? Aunt Amanda wants to meet him."

Since I wasn't fully awake yet, I blurted out, "Where?"

Her silence told me I'd screwed up, and I frantically tried to remember what I'd committed to do.

"Damnit, Libby, the concert. The orphanage. You promised you wouldn't forget."

"I didn't forget it, Nellie. I forgot today was Saturday. I'll be there, and I'll try to talk him into coming. Okay?"

"God, I can't imagine what you're gonna be like as an old lady," she said. "Try not to forget again between now and noon. And remember to get dressed unless you want to be part of the entertainment."

"What was that all about?" Dad asked when I hung up the phone.

"The charity concert for the orphanage. Nellie said

that Amanda Rollins extends a special invitation to you. She wants you to come so she can thank you."

"Well, how could I turn that down? Sure, I'll go."

I wasn't sure he would go, but I was glad to see him get out of the house. We took his car and swung by Lilith's Palace to pick up Glenda. She knew the kids at the orphanage, and a lot of the kids from the new neighborhood would be there. Mom and I thought it would be good for her to meet some normal kids.

It was the first time Glenda and Dad met, and he was entranced. Her face had filled out, and her hair had grown out enough to be shaped into a very short pixie cut. Her new jeans even showed a little teenage butt. When we arrived at the school and parked the car, I took her off to the side.

"Here are the rules. No sex, no drugs, no alcohol. If anyone makes you uncomfortable, you find me, or Dad, or Miz Rollins, or Nellie. Understand?"

Glenda nodded, her attention fixed on my face as if I were handing down the word of God.

"Don't go outside the fence. When the concert is over, find my dad. Got it?"

"Got it."

I handed her a ticket and a card with twenty creds on it. "For food. Only for you. You can buy candy and ice cream, but you have to eat at least one substantial thing. A hamburger or hot dog or poutine or chicken sandwich. Something like that. Understand?"

"Yes, ma'am."

"Go have a good time."

Her smile lit up my day. Then she lunged toward me and gave me a hug that about cracked my ribs. "I love you, Miz Libby," she said, then turned and surveyed the scene before us. My eyes were a little blurry. I must have gotten some dust in them.

They had raised a bandstand near the back of the school. A ticket stand sat just outside the fence, and inside, along the fence, were a dozen booths selling food and drink. One booth had chips with the bands' music. Additional booths showed art, jewelry and other crafts.

It was three hours before the show started, but a guy on the stage was juggling. A man and a woman in clown costumes roamed through the crowd of several hundred who were already inside.

"See Nellie over there?" I asked Glenda, trying to keep my voice steady.

"Uh-huh."

"Go ask her to introduce you to some of the kids in her family."

"Okay." She took off running.

I walked over to where Dad was watching us. "Come on. Let's find Amanda," I said.

"You're doing a good thing with that girl," he said.

"Getting her a job in a brothel?"

"A job in the kitchen. We both know what kind of mother Lettie is. Very few people get that kind of chance in life."

I shrugged.

Dad looked around. "I'm proud of you, Libby."

"I didn't do anything. This shindig is all Nellie."

"Yeah," he said, "I remember Nellie building the school with her bare hands and giving it to the orphanage. Very nice of her."

"We should name the place after Kahlil Carpenter. Come on."

I took Dad around and introduced him to Amanda

and Richard O'Malley, Nellie's corporate sugar daddy who was sponsoring the event. When we drew closer to the stage, I saw the sponsorship banners included Calderone Funeral Home.

I whirled on Nellie. "Ron is going to be here?"

"Yeah, he donated five thousand creds."

"Oh, Lord," I breathed as I looked over her shoulder and saw Wil heading toward us. "You invited Wil?"

"Honey, I invited everyone. The name of the game is money. No people, no money. If you had twenty boyfriends, I would have invited them all, but you invited Wil. Remember that night at Pinnacle?"

The crowd grew throughout the afternoon with a combination of neighborhood residents and young corporate types who would be comfortable at The Pinnacle. The Pinnacle bouncers and some of the larger men from the neighborhood provided security, but we didn't have any problems that required them to step in. Miz Rollins had nixed the idea of selling beer, and that probably helped. So did the fact that so many mothers and young children were there. Children under fourteen got in free.

While Amanda took Dad inside to show him the school, I rounded up all of the kids who lived there and herded them over to one of the booths. Amanda had twelve orphans at her old location in the slum. Now that she had room and some help, that had grown to twenty kids in a very short time.

Amanda found us just as the last kid and I received our ice cream.

"Oh, dear Lord," she said, throwing her hands in the air and glaring at me. "What are you doing? These children don't need all that sugar."

I grinned at her, handed her the sundae I was holding, and turned to the vendor. "One more, please." I turned back to Amanda. "I'm spoiling them. That's what spinster aunts do, isn't it?"

She started laughing.

Miz Libby is the best, Walter announced to the whole group. I wasn't sure if he was getting the majority of his sundae inside him, but a lot of it was smeared on his face and chest.

Things got a little awkward after Ron showed up and both he and Wil wanted to hang out with me. I started bugging Nellie to give me things to do. As the afternoon progressed and the crowd grew, it became easier to get lost. I was one of the few people allowed behind the stage, so I could effectively disappear when the music started.

I was standing off to the side of the stage when Glenda walked up and handed me a soy dog. She had one for herself, and we stood there together eating and listening to the music.

"Enjoying yourself?" I asked.

"Uh-huh. Do you know Betsy?"

I had to think a moment. "Oh, Nellie's little sister?"

"Yeah. She invited me to visit her at her house. Do you think Miz Lilith will let me go?"

"Tell her you'll do double work on your reading for a week if she lets you. She's a sucker for stuff like that." Betsy's mother was one of Mom's closest friends, so I doubted there would be a problem, but it was always good to take advantage of opportunities.

Glenda took off to find her new friend.

At the end of the night, I turned down two invitations for a drink, begging off because of Glenda and Dad. I made a note that the girl made a great excuse. I wondered how much Mom used me for an excuse when I was young. I knew she never let me get in her way when she wanted to do something.

CHAPTER 19

The following day, I arrived at the funeral home at around noon and waited. My persistence paid off. Ron fired up his motorcycle and rode off down the street soon after sunset. The funeral home and the house were completely dark, and I slipped through the shadows to a small door in the back of the building.

The door wasn't intended for people, being only a three feet high. A truck usually pulled up several times a week, and men wearing hazmat gear pulled sealed containers of biomedical waste through the door. I had watched the process that afternoon.

For my purposes, the door had only a simple latch and a single alarm contact. The security system designers had treated that entrance as an afterthought.

I bypassed the alarm contact, jimmied the latch, opened the door, and slid through. The small room opened into the embalming laboratory. From there, I knew where I was going. Making my way through the sales room, I turned into the short hallway leading to the house next door.

There weren't any caskets or anything else where I'd seen them before. I stopped and thought about everything I'd observed while watching the building.

A door at the back of the chapel led to a small warehouse filled with caskets. I searched it, but didn't find the boxes I'd seen Ron receive from Alice Alderette.

I didn't know how much time I had. Ron and I always got to his house around midnight or a little later, and it was eleven o'clock. I decided to take one more chance at finding the drugs. I didn't want him to suspect that someone was there looking for drugs, so I decided to stage a conventional burglary.

The first thing I did was disable the alarm system to the house and then short-circuit it. Next, I opened the window in a spare bedroom behind a door that was always closed. From the appearance of the room, it hadn't been used in a long time. I found the family silver, an antique brand I recognized, where I expected—in the sideboard in the dining room. It all went into a bag, and I left the drawers open. Too bad about the burglary. Karma for drug dealers.

My exit route and cover story secured, I first searched Ron's bedroom. I hadn't been with him for a while, but the wastebasket next to the bed showed someone had. I also found a ten-pack of jet injectors with four missing and a small box full of white powder. He'd never offered me drugs, but he evidently used them. I was finding it harder to remember why I wanted to date him. An antique jewelry box with what I assumed was his mother's jewelry went into the bag with the silver.

I tried the door to a room that I assumed was another bedroom. Since it was the only locked door inside the house, I immediately picked the lock to see what he was hiding there. Alice Alderette's boxes were stacked against one wall. I opened one of the boxes on the bottom of the stack and found it full of ten-packs of jet injectors. To make sure I wasn't jumping to conclusions, I took one pack for analysis, sealed the box, and stacked the other boxes back on top of it.

I slipped out the window in the spare room, jumped to the ground, and rolled. As I slipped through the shadows toward the trees on the other side of the funeral home, a single headlight appeared down the street.

I handed Wil the package of jet injectors and asked, "How soon can you get these analyzed?"

"I'll put a rush on it. We can probably get results today."

"Good. Next item, put a couple of drones on the Caldarone Funeral Home."

"Your boyfriend?"

"He's not my boyfriend. We just went out a couple of times. You want to watch for coffins shipping to anywhere other than a local cemetery. If you want to know who's distributing the drugs in other cities, track the coffins to their destinations."

Wil's eyebrows rose, but he didn't say anything.

"Then put tails on Cynthia Campbell, Alice Alderette, and Sophia Gonzales." I motioned to the jet injectors I'd given him. "Alice delivered those to Ron on Friday."

"Just these ten?"

"Nine boxes with four hundred of those ten-packs each. The outside of the boxes are printed with a brand of antacid marketed by a CanPharm subsidiary."

"Holy smokes," Wil breathed.

"Yeah. Three hundred and sixty thousand doses. Thirty-six million street value. I figure between seven and ten million split among the people making it."

Wil pulled out his phone and started issuing orders.

When he hung up, I asked, "Are you sure all your people are solid?"

"Yeah, all my staff came from out of town. People

I've worked with for years."

"I thought you lived here."

He grinned and winked. "No, Chicago. But I'm thinking about moving up here."

I wasn't so sure that was a good idea.

To help alleviate the boredom, I played the recordings from the bugs I planted on Liam Campbell. He and Cynthia were an entertaining couple. Between bouts of copulating like rabbits, they argued about sex, money, and drugs. As far as I could determine, they were made for each other. I couldn't figure out why they got divorced.

The tracker on Campbell's limo was a waste of time. His travels took him home, the office, to a few meetings at other CanPharm offices, his secretary's apartment, and the cottage he owned in the country. Wil's operatives checked out the country cottage and pronounced it clean of any covert laboratories.

The day after breaking into Ron's house, I checked my bugs right after breakfast. For a change, something was happening. I could envision the scene from what I heard.

Cynthia answered the door. "Oh, my God. What are you doing here?"

Other woman's voice. "It's so good to see you, too, my dear."

The door slammed.

"Where's Liam?" the other woman asked.

"He went to work."

"Bullshit. He went to pick up a load at the lab,

didn't he?"

"The lab's shut down. Everything went crazy."

"Don't lie to me, Cynthia. You can either tell me where it is, or I'll blow your bloody head off. Doesn't make any difference to me. When Liam comes home and sees your body, he'll know I'm serious and quit messing with me."

A woman let out a short cry. I heard someone or something bang into a piece of furniture, then the sound of someone being slammed against a wall. A woman started crying.

"I'm warning you, bitch," the unknown woman said. "You've got about ten seconds to start talking."

"Oh, God, please," Cynthia sobbed. "Please don't hurt me."

"Talk."

"The cottage."

I heard a sound that I imagined might have been Cynthia's head being slammed into the wall a couple of times.

"Don't try and pull that crap on me. I've been to the cottage. I've screwed your husband in every room. There's no lab out there."

Diane Sheridan? I'd seen pictures of her, but never heard her voice.

"The barn," Cynthia said. "About a hundred yards from the house, through the trees, is a barn. That's what he turned into a lab. He hired some grad students to make the stuff."

Silence, then, "Well, I'll be damned." More silence except for Cynthia crying.

I about jumped out of my skin when the gun went off. In the aftermath, the silence was total. Cynthia wasn't crying any more.

When I reached the Campbell's apartment building, I assumed Liam's form and let myself in. The door to the apartment itself wasn't locked.

A coffee table in the living room was askew from the other furniture, but otherwise things appeared normal. I wasn't fooled. The smell of death filled the place.

Cynthia's body lay behind the couch near the hallway to the bedrooms. She had one hole in her forehead, and a shocked expression on her face.

The Campbell's cottage was about an hour west of the city. Cottage, of course, was a relative term. I'd seen the blueprints, and the cottage was about the size of Diane Sheridan's house. I raced out to my motorcycle and headed for the freeway.

Two trucks on the freeway had some sort of computer glitch and ran into each other. Even on the bike, there wasn't room to get past. I sat and steamed for an hour waiting for the wreckage to clear. I should have asked Blaine for an aircar, even if I didn't get to keep it. By the time I got underway again, I was at least two hours behind Diane.

I left the highway and drove along the country lane that led to Campbell's cottage. About two miles away, I topped a ridge and saw smoke in the distance. By the time I reached the driveway, it was obvious my destination was the fire. Pulling into the driveway, I left the motorcycle, even though I had another half-mile to go. If the forest caught, I wanted the bike away from it.

The cottage was merrily burning, and had been for some time. The building was a total loss. I circled around and found a path through the woods.

As Cynthia said, the barn was about a hundred yards away. I expected a barn, old and big and made of wood. Instead, I found a modern one-story metal building. I drew my pistol, blurred my form, and crept closer.

The report of a pistol, one shot, sent me diving behind a tree. I crept forward, moving slowly so that I matched my surroundings. As I reached the building, I heard two more shots from inside.

I crawled around to the front door, and when I opened it, I smelled smoke, new smoke, not that of the burning house behind me. The smoke inside had more of a chemical tinge. I cautiously edged into the room and toward a hall that led farther into the building. I heard the sound of footsteps, then a door opening and closing.

Pulling on my gas mask, I cautiously worked my way through the building, but as I turned down a hall, I stopped short at the body lying there.

Liam Campbell was dead, shot three times in the torso. The smoke was getting thicker, and I didn't see any reason for me to explore farther. I made my way back outside and saw Diane Sheridan at the edge of the clearing, a pistol in her hand. She must have heard me as she turned around and raised the gun.

"You're Elizabeth Nelson, aren't you?" she called. She didn't point the gun directly at me, or make any other threatening moves.

"Yes. Diane Sheridan, I presume?"

She gave me a half-bow. "Thank you for warning my brother. Unfortunately, he went to Campbell, and that was a mistake."

"I figured you were the brains behind this operation," I said, "and now you're the only one left."

"So it seems. The brains? You flatter me. If I was smarter, I would never have let Liam talk me into it."

"Your brother invented the drugs, but Campbell was his boss. Doctor Sheridan needed you to supply test subjects. What did they talk you into? Selling it on the black market?"

"Oh, no, that was my idea, but I wanted to sell it to a different market."

I thought about it for a few moments. "More upscale. Older."

"You are a sharp girl. Yes, the yacht crowd, the investor class, the C-level society set. You could charge ten times as much per dose. You wouldn't have the distribution problems or have to split the money with so many people, so many stupid, greedy people."

"My chemist suggested that it should be diluted fifty percent," I told her. "You would be able to still charge the same amount, and not have to worry about overdoses."

She nodded. "I'll keep that in mind."

"What now?" I asked, my hand tightening on the grip of my pistol.

"I walk away, you walk away. With the lab and Campbell gone, the drug will dry up."

"There's still a lot of it out there. You could stop the deaths if you tell me who is distributing it. Besides, the genie is out. Someone will analyze it and figure out how to make it."

"Perhaps. There are a couple of tricky steps, and if you don't stabilize it properly, it deteriorates rather quickly. As to the distribution, I never wanted to know about that step. I told you, I disagreed with what they were doing."

"But you still know how to make it," I said. The building behind me was getting uncomfortably hot, and I moved away from it to my right. Diane watched me but didn't make any threatening moves.

"Oh, yes, I know how to make it. I can always rent a lab to make a batch or two. I'm not the brilliant research scientist my brother was, but I am a doctor and I am a competent lab technician. My big score, though, will be selling the final product to another drug company."

"The pills. The aphrodisiac that isn't psychoactive," I said.

"You are smart. We should get together some time."

"I don't think drugs are how I want to make my money."

"Oh, well. Good luck to you." She turned and walked away through the woods. I watched her go, then pulled out my phone, called the emergency number, and reported the fires. I figured someone should come out and make sure the forest didn't catch. There were a lot of other homes in the area.

Then I called Wil and told him about the lab and the Campbells' deaths.

CHAPTER 20

Ron called the next day and asked if I had time for lunch. That was a bit out of character.

"What's up?" I asked.

"I have a surprise for you."

Okay. It wasn't my birthday, and I doubted he was pregnant, but I decided to play along. We made arrangements to meet at a place near his home.

I parked my motorcycle and started around the corner to the café's entrance when a young woman about my age stepped in front of me. The pistol in her hand grabbed my attention. Something cold and hard and about the diameter of a pistol barrel pressed against the back of my head.

"Don't move. Don't do anything unless I tell you to," Ron said close to my ear. A hand pressed down on my shoulder. "Turn ninety degrees to your left and walk toward the car with the open door."

They hustled me into Alice Alderette's back seat, and the four of us took off. The woman I didn't recognize sat in the front seat and kept her gun pointed at me. Ron never took the muzzle of his gun away from my head.

"You don't know who I am, do you?" the woman asked.

I didn't answer.

"I'm Jennifer Blaine. You killed my father."

I knew Gareth was divorced, but I never thought to check into his children.

"You're going to tell us exactly what you're investigating, and what you told your friend Wilbur," Ron said. "Whether I give you to Jenny depends on how cooperative you are. She's very upset with you.

228

Do you understand?"

"Yes," I managed, though my mouth was so dry that it came out as a croak. I could all too easily imagine my brains splashed across the inside of that car.

I managed to beat down the panic that came close to paralyzing me and tried to envision my options. My dad and Wil were the only people I could imagine riding to my rescue. I bit down on the signal device in my mouth and prayed that Wil was paying attention.

"Start talking," Jenny said.

"What do you want to know?"

"Why did Wilberforce order drones to follow Ron and Alice?" Jenny asked.

"Because they're shipping drugs."

"Oh? And how did you find that out?" Ron asked.

"I saw her deliver them to you. I figured you're shipping them in the coffins I saw near the door that night."

Alice half-turned and spat, "You left a shipment out in the open where anyone could see it? Damn it, Ron, how stupid can you get?"

"It wasn't out in the open," he replied. "The truck was coming in the morning before we opened."

"No one could see it except whatever bimbo you dragged home that night." Jenny said.

I didn't object to being called a bimbo. As long as they didn't pull any triggers, they could call me anything they wanted to.

"Why did you order Cynthia Campbell and Sophia Gonzales followed?" Alice asked. By this time, I could see we were driving toward the funeral home, the perfect place to dispose of a body. The day was not going well.

229

"I saw you having lunch with them," I said.

Alice and Jenny exchanged a glance.

"Why were you watching my place?" Ron asked. He still hadn't relaxed, and the gun barrel still pressed against my temple.

"When I saw Sophia having lunch with Alice and Cynthia, and subsequently found out you were Brian Gonzales's cousin, I remembered those coffins with shipping labels. Then later I saw you at dinner with Sophia. Too many coincidences. I figured you were shipping the drugs, so I watched to see how you got them."

"Well, Dad was right about one thing," Jenny said. "You're definitely smarter than Wilbur. I don't think he'd have ever figured it out."

"I wish he had," I said. "I'd much rather you were pointing a gun at his head than mine."

Please, Wilbur, be listening. And hurry.

⊕⊕⊕

Ron pulled me out of the car and pushed me toward the back door of his mortuary. The last thing I wanted to do was go through that door. Joining the dead people I'd seen in there seemed like the worst idea in the world. I stumbled, put out my hand to catch myself, and pulled free from his grasp.

I rolled when I hit the ground. The report of a pistol shattered the quiet of the neighborhood, and I twisted to the side. The pistol fired again, small caliber, probably Jenny's. The bullet kicked up asphalt a few inches from me.

"Hold it right there or I'll blow your head off," Ron shouted.

230

I glanced his way and saw his gun pointed directly at me. I froze.

A shot sounded from off to my right, and Ron's head exploded. I rolled away and felt a sting in my hand as Jenny fired again. The sound of a second shot from my right coincided with Jenny spinning around and falling to the ground.

I gathered my legs under me, crouched, and readied myself to spring in any direction. Ron was obviously dead, and Jenny was out of commission. Alice stood watching with an expression of terror on her face. I leaped in her direction. She stood frozen until I almost reached her, then she turned as if to run. Wrapping my arms around her and pinning her arms to her side, I lifted her off her feet.

She kicked at me with her heels, and for the first time, I felt anger rather than fear. Two long strides took me to the building, and I slammed her into the wall, pulled back, and slammed her again. She went limp, and I let go of her, wound my left hand in her hair and punched her in the nose as hard as I could.

It felt so good that I drew my fist back to hit her again, but someone caught my arm. I whirled about in a roundhouse kick designed to knock someone's head off, but Wil ducked and blocked my foot with his forearm.

"Hey, hold on, Libby. It's over."

I glared at him, then all the adrenaline I couldn't release hit, and I started shaking. My legs gave way, and I sank to the ground next to the lump that was Alice Alderette.

Wil leaned over and took me by the arms, pulling me to my feet and wrapping me in a hug. He felt warm, and solid, and safe. Over his shoulder, I saw men with rifles and vests labeled SWAT in large yellow letters.

Someone was screaming, "Medic."

"I'm okay," I said. It was hard to talk because my teeth were chattering.

"You may be okay, but that woman is still alive." I gathered he meant Jenny. He looked down at Alice. "I think they probably need to look at her, also."

I saw a lot of blood on Alice's face.

"Bitch needed a nose job," I said, but my shaky voice made the joke fall flat.

A man with a red-cross armband walked up and said, "Let me see that hand."

I held out my right hand, the one I'd punched Alice with. I hadn't even skinned my knuckles. "It's fine." I held it up. "See?"

"I meant the other hand."

The back of my left hand had a hole in it that was pouring blood. Turning it over, I discovered a hole in the other side as well. Shards of jagged bone poked out of the hole.

"Oh. Damn! That hurts!" The world turned a little gray. I suddenly felt light-headed and swayed into Wil's chest. He helped me sit down as the medic held a jet injector to my forearm and triggered a shot. I felt immediately better, and the pain faded.

"I thought she missed me," I said.

"She almost did," the medic said, "and she almost nailed you square. Are you a glass half-empty or a glass half-full kind of girl?"

I thought about it. "I'm a grateful kind of girl." I turned my face up to Wil. "Thank you."

Wil's team searched the premises and found the drugs in the upstairs bedroom. Jennifer Blaine had taken a rifle bullet in her left shoulder. They put her in one ambulance and me in another. Alice didn't rate an ambulance. Wil said they were taking her back to Chamber headquarters and calling her husband to come get her.

"You're not letting her go, are you? What you should do is call Alonzo Donofrio to come get her."

Wil looked thoughtful.

"Call my dad and talk to him."

He nodded. "Okay. I'm still calling her husband. I think it'll be easier than hunting him down." They closed the ambulance door and made me lie down as we drove away.

⊕⊕⊕

The doctors insisted on knocking me out. I felt worse when I woke up than I did before I went to sleep.

The first thing I saw was Mom. Dad sat in his chair behind her. I croaked something and she handed me a cup full of ice chips. They tasted so good I wanted to buy the company that made them.

"How are you feeling?" Mom asked.

"Like crap. What did they do to me?"

"Anesthesia," Dad said. "You'll feel better as soon as it finishes wearing off. As for your hand, they grafted in two artificial bones, along with three muscles and two tendons from a cadaver. You're going to have about a six-month rehab before you can use it the way you used to."

I lifted the white club at the end of my left arm. "No rope climbing?"

233

"Not for a while, but the doctors said you should completely recover."

"I'm thinking of sending Glenda over to help you until you can use the hand again," Mom said. My first reaction was to say no, but then I thought about it. How many things required two hands? I decided to think about it some more before I said no.

"Well, that'll teach me to get shot. Who's paying?"

"The Chamber is," Mom said. "You're in University Hospital. The best hand surgeon in the city did the work."

I sensed someone at the door and looked up to see Wil. "Hey. It's the cavalry."

He came in the room. "You scared the hell out of me. What happened? How did they capture you?"

"Ron called and asked me to lunch. When I got there, they pulled guns on me, forced me into Alice's car, and drove me to the funeral home. I don't think they planned on letting me leave."

Wil pursed his lips. "It's my fault. You asked if the Chamber people were solid. I wasn't aware that Jennifer Blaine was in charge of the Chamber's drones. When we ordered surveillance, she knew immediately. That's why we never got any useable information."

"How is she?"

"She's out of surgery, but the doctors say she'll need at least two more procedures to fix her shoulder. It may never work properly."

"And Alice?"

He chuckled. "You broke her nose. She'll be breathing through her mouth for quite a while."

"Alonzo took her to Saint Michael's Hospital," Dad said. "He and Wil and I had a long talk. I expect

234

we'll either hear about Jimmy Alderette on the news sometime soon, or we'll never hear about him again. As for Alice and Sophia, let's just say that Alonzo wasn't pleased."

"So where does that leave us? Do we know who was distributing the drugs in the other cities? Did the women talk?"

Dad and Wil exchanged an unhappy glance. "No," Wil said, "we didn't get a chance to interrogate Alice and Sophia. We're hoping Jennifer Blaine will talk."

"Alonzo said he'd let us know if Sophia or Alice know anything," Dad said.

⊕⊕⊕

I'd been in the hospital for a week, and then home for ten days, when the doctor reduced the bandages by a couple of pounds. The hand was still tender, and hurt if I banged it against anything, but I could finally use it to drive. Mom loaned me her car, since she could use any of the three chauffeured limos she owned. I took Glenda out into the country for a picnic. It was the first time in her life to cross the city boundaries of Toronto.

The main purpose of the car, though, was to reach my daily physical therapy appointments. After a week, I was convinced the sweet young therapist was really the last surviving member of the Inquisition.

"Oh," she said brightly when I complained, "you thought PT meant physical therapist? You almost got it right. It stands for physical terrorist." And then she laughed.

I spent a lot of our sessions fantasizing painful ways for her to die.

I discovered a lot of things required two hands. Washing my hair for one thing. Dresses were a lot easier than pants, but zipping up could be a problem so I had to choose dresses without back zippers. No shoes with laces. Cooking required two hands, especially for chopping things. That wouldn't normally be a problem, since I never cooked, but Glenda insisted on showing off her new skills. The kid did a pretty good job with basic stuff. She made a dynamite pizza and some tasty pastries.

Something she couldn't help with was the computers. I typed fast enough to take dictation on a keyboard, so typing with one hand was frustrating. Voice commands were fine for simple things, but the kind of computer commands I used required a finer touch. The infonet was the only thing that kept me from going totally stir crazy, though. I spent a lot of time teaching Glenda basic computer skills and helping her read the stuff she found online.

The workmen completed the repairs on Dad's house, and he moved back home. He came over a couple of times a week to help Glenda cook, and shuttled her to the grocery store and me to doctor's appointments. Watching Glenda in a grocery store was an experience. The first time, she just stood and stared, not sure where to start.

Wil dropped by almost every day to update me on the investigation. Jimmy Alderette and his wife completely dropped out of sight. Wil did say that Sophia flew out on her father's plane to Italy, evidently for a long vacation. Otherwise, the Donofrio family was a black hole as far as information. Total silence.

⊕⊕⊕

The doorbell rang. "I'll get it, Glenda," I called.

I opened the door to find Wil standing there.

"Oh, hi. What's up?" I asked.

"I dropped by to see if you wanted to go to dinner. I'm headed back to Chicago in the morning."

"You really should have called," I said. "I'd love to go with you, but tonight isn't good. Glenda cooked her first lasagna, and we invited people over." Nellie and my mom and dad were there. "You're welcome to eat with us. Are you sure you couldn't stay over another day?"

He bit his lip and took a deep breath. "No, I already told my boss I'd be back in Chicago tomorrow."

"Give me a call the next time you're in town?"

"I'll do that," Wil said. He turned to walk away, then turned back. "I do want to see you again."

I watched him walk back to his car. I wondered if he was serious about moving to Toronto.

###

If you enjoyed **Chameleon Assassin**, I hope you will take a few moments to leave a brief review on the site where you purchased your copy. It helps other readers when you share your experience. Potential readers depend on comments from people like you to help guide their purchasing decisions. Thank you for your time!

Get updates on new book releases, promotions, contests and giveaways! Sign up for my newsletter.

Coming soon in early 2017
(sneak peek starts on the next page)

Chameleon Uncovered

Other books by BR Kingsolver

The Telepathic Clans Saga

The Succubus Gift
Succubus Unleashed
Broken Dolls
Succubus Rising
Succubus Ascendant

BRKingsolver.com

CHAMELEON UNCOVERED

CHAPTER 1

An aircar rose from the roof. Soon after, most of the lights in the penthouse above the twenty-second floor went out. Time for me to go to work.

My chameleon abilities allowed me to blend into the shadows as I crossed the road. In a lot of ways, I would rather break into a walled estate than a high-rise apartment building. During the day, when Fredrick Olson was at work, his mistress and the housekeeper were home. In the evening, most of the other residents throughout the building were home and the place was crawling with personal security personnel, also known as bodyguards.

On a previous foray into the building, I learned that some of Olson's security guards remained on duty when he went out. That eliminated the easy way in. Climbing a twenty-two-story building was a difficult proposition at the best of times, but I was recovering from a bullet wound and surgery to my left hand. Climbing anything was beyond my current capabilities.

The deepest shadows lay between the last row of balconies on the southwest side of the building and the corner of the building closest to the lake. If I kept completely still, even the security cameras couldn't pick me up. I had to move, though, to reach my destination.

An arm's length from the wall, I turned on the personal jetpack I wore and rose until I reached the roof. I never could have afforded such a toy, but on a previous job, I couldn't resist taking it, along with the painting I was commissioned to acquire. My client paid me handsomely, but far less than he had offered the painting's owner. Watching the rich and infamous play games with each other diminished much of my desire for material wealth.

I pulled myself onto the roof and lay between the parapet and the greenhouse glass, barely breathing, waiting for some kind of alarm. Nothing happened.

Shrugging out of the jetpack harness, I looked around. The penthouse covered half the roof. I knew that the Olson apartment also included the entire floor below me. A domed greenhouse with a garden covered the other half of the roof. From below, the dome wasn't visible, but I had assumed it was there. The palm trees looked much too healthy to be exposed to unfiltered city air.

I crawled along until I reached the gardener's shed. As far as I could tell, it was the only door from inside the dome to the outside. The door had an electronic combination lock, and had a simple alarm contact, but that was it. I bypassed the alarm and disabled the lock. When I pulled on the door, I discovered it wasn't used very often. Creaking, rusty hinges screamed and I winced. Sticking my head inside the room was impossible. Twenty-liter buckets of fertilizer were stacked higher than my head against the door.

A panicked glance at the house showed no movement or change. I was hoping no one was inside the apartment. If so, I was already screwed. As quietly and carefully as I could, I pulled enough plastic buckets of one stack down out to create an opening and restacked them against the shed by the door. It took a few minutes, but I managed to clear a space I could squeeze through. My night-vision goggles showed me a neat little room with tools and various buckets and bins and a wheelbarrow.

Another door opened into the garden, which had a glass ceiling about thirty feet overhead. I seriously doubted security cameras or pressure sensors covered the space. Why bother? Breaking through the acrylic glass would take a bomb. I knew it was designed to withstand tree limbs being blown into it at over sixty miles an hour.

Keeping low and blending into the shadows, I made my way past a fountain to an area with several tables surrounded by chairs. No one sat outside enjoying sunny days anymore, at least not in the city, but if you were rich, evidently you could pretend.

The sliding-glass door from the garden to the house didn't have an alarm contact on it. It wasn't even locked. I just walked right in to an entertainment area with a bar, dance floor, and more tables and chairs. Beyond was a formal dining room and a small kitchen.

The rooftop level was primarily for entertainment, including a game room, and a gymnasium with a lap pool. I took the servant's stairs from the small kitchen down to the main level.

According to Evelyn Olson, the woman who hired me, the jewelry would be in a safe in the master bedroom. I'd spent the previous week scouting the job, following the mark and mapping his habits and movements. But it all came down to sitting outside the exclusive apartment building, topped by Fredrick Olson's penthouse overlooking the lake, and waiting for him and his arm candy to head out for a see-and-be-seen charity event. The kind of event where the richer-than-God set got together and donated fifteen minutes' income and gave fifteen minutes' lip service to the "unfortunate among us."

Evelyn was lucky her pre-nuptial agreement prevented Fredrick from just dumping her on the street. Corporate marriages sometimes resembled royal marriages in ages past, a means of cementing alliances and creating acceptable babies. Negotiating teams for the pre-nups occasionally employed dozens of lawyers. Evelyn was from a prominent corporate family, and her pre-nup evidently was airtight. But her husband had taken all her jewelry when he left.

Dad always told me to be careful about getting involved with domestic disputes. I understood the potential problems, but it was hard to turn down a hundred grand for one night's work. I still was skeptical until Evelyn showed me two pictures, one of her grandmother wearing a necklace, and then a picture of Fredrick's sixteen-year-old sugar baby wearing the necklace. I'm about as cynical as they come, but fair is fair.

Fredrick Olson's new playmate was a scandal. She was undeniably beautiful, but too young, too uneducated, and too middle-class to fit into corporate society properly. No one would have blinked if he wanted to keep the kid as his mistress, maybe not even Evelyn, but he wanted a divorce so he could marry the kid. Upper-class society was completely aghast.

I found the safe, and the combination was still the same as the one Evelyn gave me. I took the jewelry that matched the insurance pictures she had shown me and put the rest back. Evelyn wanted to send a message. I felt a little guilty, though. The gig was almost too easy.

If I were working for myself, a lot of the artwork and the rest of the jewelry would have been in jeopardy. Since Evelyn planned on flaunting the jewelry, I made every effort to leave everything exactly as I found it.

But what were the chances that Fredrick would miss a half-dozen bottles of wine and whiskey? On my way out, I looked into the wine cellar and under the bar. I wasn't a real expert in fancy alcohol, so I checked his stock against the infonet and found the most expensive wines for Mom and the most expensive whiskey for Dad. It never hurt to butter up the parents in case I needed a favor.

Stacking the fertilizer back in place finished the job and I rode the jetpack down to the ground.

⊕⊕⊕

Evelyn and I met for lunch the next day at a charming little bistro that catered to the money-is-no-object crowd. I didn't object since the menu proudly boasted that the fish contained no heavy metals or toxins, and she was paying.

We did the so-good-to-see-you air-kiss thing and I passed her a shopping bag. "Happy birthday!"

"Oh, you shouldn't have," she said, slipping me a payment card worth a hundred thousand credits.

"I recovered all the pieces except one," I told her after the waiter took our orders. "The diamond and turquoise choker."

"The little slut probably wore it," Evelyn said with a shrug. "Such is life. At least you got my grandmother's necklace and the antique diamond set." She grinned. "I'm going to love seeing Fredrick's face at the museum fund raiser when I wear them."

I chuckled. "Who are you going with?" A man I was dating had invited me, and it suddenly looked as though it might be more interesting than I'd thought.

"Margaret Channing and her brother," Evelyn said. "You know I don't dare go near a man until the divorce is final. It's fine for him to screw around, but he would love to invoke the infidelity clause in the pre-nup."

"Seems like a silly clause since you didn't have any children," I said.

"Definitely. It turns out that he's sterile." She gave an aggrieved sigh. "You know, Elizabeth, before the world went to hell in a hand basket, there was a movement in North America and Europe that came close to giving women true equality with men. But as soon as the corporations took over, the boys at the top put a stop to that."

I'd read about that in my history classes at the university. It wasn't that women were denied equality, but at the top of the social ladder, women such as Evelyn and her mother, and my maternal grandmother, surrendered equality in favor of the comfort and luxury their beauty could buy. Very few women cracked the top levels of corporate hierarchies.

Nothing stopped Evelyn from going out and starting her own company. But instead of going to university when she was eighteen, she had married a corporate executive eighteen years her senior. I didn't have a lot of sympathy for her, since she was Olson's second wife. He seemed to trade them in when they hit thirty-two.

We ate our lunches, gossiping like a normal pair of corporate trophy wives. After we parted, I went to the ladies' room and changed my appearance, morphing from the woman Evelyn knew into plain old me. With an extra eight inches of height, the knee-length dress looked a bit more risqué, appropriate for a woman ten years younger than the woman Evelyn knew. I never wore my real face to meet a mark. I always sought to avoid unexpected knocks on the door late at night. Some people have no sense of humor when their heirlooms disappear.

CPSIA information can be obtained
at www.ICGtesting.com
Printed in the USA
FSHW022004310121
78205FS